She slapped him with all her might. And then it came with a rush . . . From childhood the great flaw in his make-up had been his temper. It had been a hair-trigger thing, exploding at his governess, the servants, other children, his mother. . . . Now Sheila's hot words, his own guilt, the underlying fear of the confrontation with his father, made him erupt. He leaped at Sheila, whirled her about, and seized her by the throat. Sheila struggled; her resistance fed his fury. His fingers tightened. . . . It was not until her face turned livid, her cries became gurgles, her eyes glassed over—it was not until then that . . .

The Fourth Side of the Triangle

Ellery Queen

BALLANTINE BOOKS • NEW YORK

.BALLANTINE BOOKS
A Division of Random House, Inc.
201 East 50th Street, New York, N.Y. 10022
Simultaneously published by
Ballantine Books, Ltd., Toronto, Canada

Contents

I. The First Side

SHEILA

That oozing Tuesday in August, Dane was planning his weekend. The choices were several. He was invited to a party the guiding idea of which was to charter a canalboat in Newcastle, Pennsylvania, and glide through Bucks County watching the south end of the mule head north along the towpath (or was it the north end heading south?), lallygagging around under the awning away from the gassy streets of the metropolitan summer. It was tempting to contemplate a floating journey through a tunnel of cool green trees; and afterward, in the evening, fireflies, lanterns on lawns, and dancing.

Or there was the invitation to join friends on Fire Island; the swimming would be better (Dane liked surf), and the trip was shorter.

A third choice lay up the Hudson, at an estate near Rhinebeck. It meant a pool for swimming (Dane detested pools), and the nuisance of formal dress; but the food would be superb, and one or two of the women, too.

Of one thing he was certain: wherever he wound up, it was not going to be in New York, broiling to death. No matter what.

But there was a matter.

Because this was before he found out about his father.

The first McKell had come to America while New York was still Nieuw Amsterdam, following a small disagreement with the Laird of the Clan. It was with some disquiet that the disgruntled immigrant subsequently observed the royal banner of the Stuarts waving over his city of refuge, Peter Stuyvesant not to the contrary; but the Duke of York and his lieutenants seemed not to be interested in any affront offered The McKell by his hot-tempered cousin. Gradually he came out of retreat;

cautiously he began to buy a little and sell a little, to export and import in a modest way. This founding McKell took a wife, begat progeny, and died in the Presbyterian faith, leaving an estate of £500 and the advice, "Be aye canny wi' sil'er and dinna spend it saftly." His eldest son took the pioneer's advice to heart so earnestly that he was reputed never to spend sil'er at all. In any case, the son left £1000 in the family strongbox and a sloop in the Hudson River.

So it had gone, McKell outdoing McKell in enterprise and thrift. During the Civil War the reigning McKell, one James, proved the man for the time. James hired a substitute in the draft, took contracts to supply the Union Army with black walnut wood for riflestocks, died seized of an apoplexy, and left almost $1,000,000. James's son Taylor, having no war available in which to test his patriotism, exercised his energies by expanding the family trade in sugar, coffee, and tobacco. He also had the foresight to invest in shipping in a period when the American merchant marine was still a sludge of wreckage from the damage done by Confederate raiders and railroad competition. He died at a vast age, leaving over $3,000,000, a young son named Ashton, and a pew in New York's Grace Episcopal Church.

Ashton McKell was in his mid-fifties when his son Dane made the seismic discovery about him. Many of Ashton's contemporaries had failed even to maintain their original inheritances, blaming the unions, the income tax, the crash, and that Traitor to His Class for their misfortune. Not so Ashton McKell. Ashton had doubled his portion before he was twenty-five, and then doubled that. And more. The ships of the McKell Lines sailed every sea. There was McKell coffee, supplied (under various brand names) to more American homes than the competition looked upon with happiness; and the coffee was more often than not sweetened with McKell sugar (no retail sales). And the cigarets inhaled afterward were certain to contain the products of the National & Southern Tobacco Company (a wholly owned McKell subsidiary). The combined worth of Ashton McKell's interests came to something between $80,- and $100,000,000; even Ashton was not quite sure.

3

And he still had the first shilling the first McKell in America had ever turned over to a profit.

"Dane," said Lutetia McKell. "There is something I must tell you about your father."

Ashton's drive was all thrust. "Take it easy?" he had once snorted to his doctor. "If I had it in me to take it easy, I'd have been clipping coupons for the past twenty years. Do you call that living?"

Not for him the slow life terminating in the long death. He liked to recall Zachary McKell. Old Zach had dropped in his tracks at the age of ninety-two after cutting the winter's wood rather than pay a sawyer the outlandish fee of $1.00 a cord to do it for him.

"Moderation be damned" was Ashton's credo. He smoked twenty cigars a day, ate rich and fatty foods, worked, played, and fought hard; in the chart room of his empire he delegated as little real authority as he efficiently could.

Dane was very like his father in appearance. He had inherited the high color, the Caesarean nose, the imperial chin, the wavy brown hair women liked to stroke. But where the father's eyes were the chill gray of his ancestors from "the bleak and difficult Hebrides," the son's were the china-blue of his mother's. And the clusters of muscle at the corners of Ashton's mouth were missing from Dane's except when Dane flew into one of his rages.

"Mother!" Dane sprang from the chair, pretending a surprise he did not really (and this was curious) feel. "Are you dead sure? I can't believe it."

But he could.

4

Ashton's doubts about his son were of long standing. They had been born in Dane's childhood. A boy who preferred books to football! Mendelssohn to "Old Man River" (and later, Mozart to Mendelssohn)! Languages to Math! Comparative Religion to Economics! Ancient History to Business Administration! Coin collecting to coin amassing! What kind of McKell had he spawned?

The father told himself that it was all "a phase," like Dane's incredible preference (at the appropriate age) for poetry over whorehouses. "He'll grow out of it," Ashton McKell kept saying. When Dane was in private school, his father was confident that prep school would "change" him. Groton having failed, perhaps Yale would succeed. Privately Ashton held that a hitch in the Marine Corps might prove a likelier agency, but of course the very idea could not be breathed to Lutetia, who considered the National Registration Act an affront to decent people. Dane continued to hack out his own trail.

For all his misgivings, Ashton McKell never once envisioned the worst. Dane dropped out of Yale, disappeared. His father found him toiling under a beefy sun in one of North Carolina's tobacco plantations—not even McKell-owned! Later he took a job as a deck hand on one of the McKell freighters. But he jumped ship in Maracaibo, and turned up six months later in a Greenwich Village pad, shacked up with a long-haired girl with dirty bare feet and oil paint on her nose. He spent the better part of another year riding the rods and bunking down in hobo jungles; in the space of the following three years he was a Hollywood extra, a carny roustabout, buddy-buddy with a gang of *braceros* down around the Mexican border, a beach boy at Santa Monica, a field hand on a Hawaiian pineapple plantation, and legman for an alcoholic Chicago police reporter who needed somebody to keep him from being rolled and perhaps knifed in a Loop alley.

When Dane showed up at home, lean and hungry-looking as Cassius (his mother spent three marvelous months cooking for him with her own hands—a service, Ashton remarked wryly, that she had never rendered to *him*), his father said, "Every McKell for centuries has gone into the family business."

"I," said Dane, "am breaking the chain."

It was as if he had announced that he was en route to the Trappist monastery in Kentucky to take the vows of silence.

"You mean you're *not?*"

"Why should I, Dad? I don't like business. Any business. Yours included . . . Anyway, it isn't as if I had to." Dane was on the pale side, but the McKell chin was noticeably firm.

"What in hell do you mean by that?" Ashton shouted. Silence swallowed the shout.

At least, the father thought, he's not being flip about it. He realizes what this damned radical nonsense means . . . Ashton could not have endured it if the boy had been casual.

"I'm of age," Dane said. "It doesn't mean merely that I now have the vote and can join the lodge. Grandfather McKell and Grandfather DeWitt both made provision for me in their wills, Dad. What do I need business for?"

"You mean to say you intend to live without working? By God, Dane, that's cheap—I mean, cheap!"

"I didn't mean that at all. I'm going to work. But it's work of my choice . . . In a way," Dane said thoughtfully, "I didn't choose it so much as it chose me."

Ashton McKell did not live by bread alone. He was a confident communicant of his faith, and a vestryman. This rushed into his head. Appalled, he cried, "You're going into the Church?"

"What? No." Dane laughed. "I'm going to write."

There was a blank space. Then Ashton said, "Well, I don't think I understand. Write? Write what?"

A *writer?*

Ashton probed his memory. Had he ever known a writer? Known anyone who knew a writer? There was Lamont's son Corliss, but he was a Socialist. And that young Vanderbilt, Cornelius—he hadn't even had *that* excuse. And . . . yes, his late mother's friend, Mrs. Jones, who had written novels under her maiden name of Edith Wharton. But—damn it all!—she had been a woman.

"So you're going to write," Ashton said slowly, and he asked again, "Write what?" searching his mind for a sensible explanation. He fell on one: his mother. His mother spoiled him.

"Fiction. Novels, principally," Dane said. "I've already dipped my toes in the short story—one was published in a little magazine; I don't suppose you found time to read it in the copy I sent you." Dane smiled faintly. "I'm lucky. I mean, having the means to write without having to worry about rent money or the electric bill—or, for that matter, deadlines. A lot of writers have to write stuff they loathe, just to keep the fuel pump going. I don't have to do that—"

"Because of money you didn't earn," said his father.

"I admitted I'm lucky, Dad. But I hope to justify my luck by producing good books." Dane saw his father's look and said carefully, "Don't get me wrong. Supplying people with sugar and coffee is honorable employment—"

"Thanks!" Ashton said sarcastically. Nevertheless, he was touched. At least, he said to himself, the boy doesn't accuse me of being a rotten capitalist exploiter or sneer at the way his people have been making a living for almost three hundred years.

"Only it's not for me, Dad. I'm going to write. I want to. I have to."

"Well," said Ashton McKell. "We'll see."

He saw. He saw that it was neither phase nor fancy, but good solid ambition.

Dane took an apartment of his own in one of the buildings he had inherited from the estate of Gerard DeWitt. He did this with kindness, and for a long time scarcely a day passed without a visit home; but Ashton knew that it was not so much from genuine involvement as out of consideration for his mother's feelings.

The boy worked hard, his father had to concede. Dane allowed himself exactly one weekend off each month; the rest was four walls, stuffy cigaret smoke, and the firing of his typewriter. He wrote, rewrote, destroyed, started over.

His first novel, *Hell in the Morning*, was a flop utter and absolute. No major reviewer mentioned it, and the minor ones were merciless. A typical notice from a provincial book column said: "*Hell in the Morning* is hell any time of the day." He was scolded as "a rich man's Nelson Algren" and "Instant Kerouac" and "a moth in the beard of Steinbeck." One lady reviewer ("Why doesn't she stay home and wash the dirty diapers?" roared Ashton McKell) remarked: "Rarely has such small talent labored so hard to produce so little." Dane, who had been absorbing punishment like an old club fighter, in grim silence, cried out when he read that one. But his father (only Judith Walsh, Ashton's private secretary, knew that the tycoon had subscribed to a clipping service) stormed and raved.

"The Duxbury *Intelligencer!* What's that smelly little rag good for but to wrap codfish in?" and so on. Finally, anger spent, came consolation. "At least now he'll give up this tomfoolery."

"Do you think so, Ashton?" Lutetia asked. It was at one of the family dinners from which Dane was absent —his absences were becoming more frequent. It was clear that Lutetia did not know whether to be sorry for her son's sake or glad for her husband's. The struggle, as usual, was short-lived. "I hope so, dear," Lutetia said. If Ashton thought writing was bad for Dane, it was.

"I simply don't understand you people." Judy Walsh was a more than occasional visitor to her employer's home. Ashton required outlandish hours of his secretary, sometimes dictating well past midnight in his study, so that Judy was frequently there for dinner. She was important to Lutetia McKell in another way. Lutetia's never-expressed regret had been for lack of female companionship. Her few nieces were too emancipated for her taste, and there was Judy, an orphan, trim, efficient, outspoken, and yet, under the independence, with a need no one but Lutetia suspected, a need like her own, feminine, and yearning for tenderness. Judy's hair bordered on Irish red, and she had a slanty little Irish nose and direct blue Irish eyes. "Really, Mr. McKell." Thus

Judy, at Ashton's remark. "Give up this tomfoolery! You sound like a character out of the Late Late Show. Don't you know enough about Dane to realize he won't ever give up?"

Ashton growled into his soup.

Dane's second novel, *The Fox Hunters*, was a failure also. The *Times* called it "Faulkner and branch water, New England style." *The New Yorker* said *(in toto):* "A teen-ager's first experience with Life turns out to be not at all what he had thought. Callow." The *Saturday Review* . . .

Dane continued to plow away.

It turned out to be the kind of New York August which made it technically possible to walk from back to peeling back at Coney Island, from the boardwalk to the sea, without once touching the scorched sand. It was the season when mild little men who had never been known to raise their voices ran through the streets slashing at people with an ax . . . when those New Yorkers who owned no air-conditioners used fans, and those who owned no fans slept on kitchen floors before open refrigerators, so that the overloaded circuits blew out, nullifying refrigerators, fans, and air-conditioners alike.

Tempers erupted, gangs rumbled, husbands slugged their wives, wives beat their children, offices closed early, subways re-enacted the Inferno, in the thick and dripping air hearts faltered and gave up the blood-pumping struggle, and Lutetia McKell told her son that his father had confessed to her: "There is another woman."

"Mother!" Dane sprang from the chair, pretending a surprise he did not really feel. "Are you dead sure? I can't believe it."

But he could. Queer. A moment before his mother said, "There is another woman," Dane could have said in truth that the thought of his father's possible infidelity had never crossed his mind. Yet once the words were uttered, they seemed inevitable. In common with most of mankind, Dane could not think comfortably of his parents in sexual embrace; but in his case the Freudian reasons were complicated by the kind of father and mother he had. His mother was like a limpet clinging to a rock, getting far more than she gave; for she could only give acquiescence and loyalty as she moved up and down with the tides. Somewhere deep in his head flickered the thought: she must be the world's lousiest bed partner.

It seemed obvious to Dane that his father, on the other hand, was a man of strong sexuality, in common with his other drives and appetites. The surprise lay not so much in the fact that there was another woman as in that he had been so blind.

So—"Are you dead sure? I can't believe it."—when he was certain from the first instant, and belief came flooding.

"Oh, yes, I'm sure, darling," said Lutetia. "It's not the sort of thing I would imagine." No, Dane thought; you'd far likelier imagine a Communist revolution and a commissar commandeering your best silver service. "But for some time now I've . . . well, suspected something might be wrong."

"But, Mother, how did you find out?"

Lutetia's cameo face turned rosy. "I asked him what was wrong. I could no longer stand thinking all sorts of things."

"What did he say?" So you do lead a mental life, Dane thought, after all. Funny, finding out about one's parents at such an advanced stage of the game. He loved his mother dearly, but he would have said she hadn't a brain in her head.

"He said, 'I'm terribly sorry. There is another woman.' "

"Just like that?"

"Well, dear, I asked him."

"I know, but—! What did *you* say?"

"What could I say, Dane? I've never been faced with such a situation. I think I said, 'I'm sorry, too, but it's such a relief to know,' which it was. Oh, it was."

"And then what did Dad say, do?"

"Nodded."

"*Nodded?* That's all?"

"That's all." His mother said, as he winced, "I'm sorry, darling, but you did ask me."

"And that was the end of the conversation?"

"Yes."

Incredible. It was like something out of Noel Coward. And now Dane realized something else. Just below the level of consciousness he had been aware lately of an aura of disturbance about his mother. It probably accounted for his uneasiness and reluctance to leave the city. Her dependence on her menfolk was bred into his bones.

As Dane once joked to Judy Walsh, his mother represented a species perhaps not quite so extinct—if there were degrees of extinction—as the heath hen, the passenger pigeon, or the Carolina parakeet, but rarer than the buffalo.

Anna Lutetia DeWitt McKell was an atavism. Born six years after Queen Victoria's death, Lutetia in her single delicate body carried the Victorian spirit into the middle of the twentieth century, nursing it as if she were the divinely appointed guardian of the eternal flame. It was true that, being left motherless, she had been reared by a coker-collared grandmother who was by birth a Phillipse, and who never let anyone, especially Lutetia, forget it; the old lady considered herself spiritually, at least, a daughter of England (the Phillipses were Tories during the Revolution); she never failed to take offense at being called an Episcopalian—"I am an Anglican Catholic," she would say. But the grandmother did not entirely explain the granddaughter. On the paternal side Lutetia inherited all the pride and prejudices of the ingrown Knickerbocker breed from which her father's family descended. Between the Victorian and Dutch burgher virtues, Lutetia never had a chance.

Secretly, she still considered it "wrong" for young people of opposite sexes to be left alone together under any circumstances; the social freedom of the twentieth century bewildered and offended her. The very word "sex" was not used in "mixed" conversation by "ladies"; it had taken all her strength to utter the phrase "another woman" in the conversation with her son. There were other social distinctions as well in Lutetia's lexicon. Judith Walsh, for example, was "a business associate" of her husband's (and what a wrench it was for her to acknowledge that "a nice young woman" could be engaged in "business"!); had she had to think of Judy as an employee, Lutetia would inescapably have lumped her with the "servant class." One always spoke politely, even kindly, to servants; but one did not, after all, dine with them.

Lutetia DeWitt had led the proper sheltered life; she had attended the proper young ladies' schools; she had made the grand tour properly chaperoned; she had never been inside a night club (Lutetia called it a "cabaret") in her life (a night club, after all, was a sort of saloon). She sipped a glass a sherry on occasion; beer she regarded as a food, which might be drunk for the purpose of gaining weight; whiskey was exclusively for men. She liked to devote at least one hour a day to her "needlework," but this was never worked on in the presence of callers because it consisted of "tiny garments," prepared for a lay sisterhood of her church which aided "unfortunate" young women.

She was, as Dane remarked to Judy, beyond belief. "I love Mother," he said, "but to be in her company for any length of time is like living onstage during a performance of *Berkeley Square*."

"Dane! What a thing to say."

"I've had to live with her, Judykins."

Divorced women who remarried were living in adultery; there was no more to be said on the subject, except of course that one was sorry for their unhappy children.

It was in the area of sex and marriage that Lutetia McKell's upbringing expressed itself most strongly. A woman came to her marriage bed a virgin; the mere contrary thought was unspeakable. She would no more have thought of taking a lover than of allowing herself to be eaten by bears. Twin beds were as alien to her as prayer rugs or cuspidors, although separate bedrooms served certain marital situations. She knew dimly that in

12

the unmapped seas in which husbands moved, there were such monsters as "loose women," for each of whom there had to be a philandering man; in a vague way, while she disapproved, she also accepted. In this sense Lutetia McKell was far more middle-class French than upper-class English or American.

That she possessed an independent fortune was a felicity, a convenience that meant she had the means to indulge in private charities and bestow personal gifts. For family and domestic expenses she did not handle a penny or sign a check, and it had never occurred to her to demand the right as a matter of wifehood.

Lutetia McKell lived where her husband decreed, traveled when, as, and where he stipulated, bought what he told her to buy, ran her home as he wanted it run. She was happy when her husband seemed content; she grieved when he was out of sorts. She had no significant hopes or desires that were not Ashton McKell's, and she felt no lack of any.

Still . . . "another woman" . . .

Why, the old goat, Dane thought.

Most deeply, he felt sorry for his mother; on another level, not so deep, he felt rather sorry for his father. But it was his mother who preoccupied him. How could she cope with a situation for which she had no background or resources? She was not like other women.

"It's never happened before," she said, and her lips compressed ever so slightly, as if to say, *And it should not have happened now;* but the lip compression was as far as the criticism would ever get. "I know that men have, well, certain *feelings* that women may not have, and there are undoubtedly situations in which they— you—cannot control yourselves absolutely. But with your father it's never happened before, Dane, I'm quite certain of that." It was as if she were pleading her husband's case before some attentive court. She sat in her chair with hands lapped over, no hint of tears in her childlike blue eyes—a fragile figure of middle-aged porcelain.

13

He shouldn't have done it to her. Dane ruminated. Not to Mother. She's not equipped. Regardless of the deficiencies of their intimate life together, he shouldn't have made her a victim of this commonest of marital tragedies. Not after living with her all these years. Not after taking her little Victorian self as it was and molding it to his accommodation. What did she have without her husband? Ashton McKell was her reason for being. It left her like a planet torn loose from its sun. Dane began to feel angry.

It made him re-examine himself, because at first he had been inclined to see it through male eyes. What might it be like to visit a father's home and find some brittle, dyed creature in her sharp-featured forties . . . "Dane, this is your stepmother." "Oh, Ashie, no! You call me Gladys, Dane." Or Gert, or Sadie. Dane shivered. Surely his father couldn't have fallen that low. Not some brassy broad out of a night-club line.

"Mother, has he said anything about a divorce?"

Lutetia turned her clear eyes on him in astonishment. "Why, what a question, Dane. Certainly not! Your father and I would never consider such a thing."

"Why not? If—"

"People of our class don't get divorces. Anyway, the Church doesn't recognize divorce. I certainly don't want one, and even if I did your father wouldn't dream of it."

I'll bet, Dane thought grimly. He forbore to point out what Lutetia perfectly well knew—that so long as neither of the parties remarried after a civil divorce, no rule of the Episcopal Church was broken. But how could she stand for the adultery? To his surprise, Dane discovered that he was taking an old-fashioned view of his own toward the disclosure. Or was it simply that he was putting himself in his mother's place? (All at once, the whole problem became entangled. He found himself thinking of the McKell money. The McKell money meant nothing to him, really—he had never particularly coveted it, he had certainly not earned a cent of it, with his two inheritances he did not need any part of it, and he had repeatedly refused to justify his legatee status in respect to it. Yet now the thought that the bulk of it might wind up the property of "another woman" infuriated him.)

"He's cheated on you, Mother. How can you go on living with him?"

"I'm surprised at you, Dane. Your own father."

She was ready to forgive adultery. Did the drowning woman refuse the life preserver because it was filthy with oil scum? Lutetia sat patiently on a chair which a young male favorite of *le roi soleil's* brother had given to his own female favorite—sat patiently and unaware of this aspect of the chair's history—and stared without seeing it at a painting of the Fontainebleau school in which rusty nymphs languished under dark trees . . . a painting hanging where the portrait had hung of her Grandmother Phillipse, dressed in the gown she had worn on being presented to "Baron Renfrew" a century ago.

"I would give your father a divorce, of course," she went on in her "sensible" voice, "if he wanted it. But I'm sure the thought has never crossed his mind. No McKell has ever been divorced."

"Then why in God's name did he tell you about this at all?" demanded Dane, exasperated.

Again the faintly reproving look. "Please don't take the name of the Lord in vain, darling."

"I'm sorry, Mother. Why did he?"

"Your father has never kept secrets from me."

He resisted an impulse to fling up his hands, and instead walked over to the big window to stare out at Park Avenue.

Dane was not fooled by his mother's assertion of faith. His father had kept plenty of secrets from her. If he really didn't want a divorce, it was because he wasn't in love with the woman. And this made Dane even angrier. It meant that it was a cheap passing affair, a meaningless tumble in the bed, for the sake of which the old bull was ready to give infinite pain to his wife and face the possibility of a dirty little scandal in the sensational press if the story should leak out.

Poor Mother! Dane thought. Up to now the nearest she's come to scandal has been at fifth or sixth remove; now here it is just around the corner. *A lady's name appears in a newspaper three times in her life: when she is born, when she marries, and when she dies.* To this

15

quaint credo Lutetia subscribed completely. Didn't she realize what she was facing? He turned from the window and said something to this effect.

"I had naturally thought about that," Lutetia said, nodding. Was there a flicker of something in the depths of those blue eyes? "And I mentioned it to your father. He assures me that there is no chance anyone will ever find out. He is apparently being very discreet. Taking special precautions of some sort, I believe."

I *am* awake, Dane said to himself, this is *not* a dream. They had discussed the cheating husband's precautions against being found out, and let it go at that! It made his father almost as unbelievable as his mother. Or had Ash McKell become so accustomed to twisting her to his every whim that he now had nothing but contempt for her? Have I ever understood my mother and father? Dane wondered; and he was struck by the predicament of modern man, not merely unable to communicate but, oftener than not, ignorant of the fact.

Talk about faithful Griselda! The heroine of the Clerk's Tale was flaming with rebellion compared to his mother. She had devoted her life so single-mindedly to the happiness of her husband that she even went along with his betrayal of her as a woman! Or does that make me some sort of Buster Brown-haired prig? Dane thought. Considered as a feat of character, there was actually something sublime in Lutetia's meekness. Maybe it's I who haven't grown up.

"Mother." His tone was gentle. "Who is she? Do you know? Did he tell you?"

Again she surprised him. This descendant of a hundred Knickerbockers smiled her sweet and self-effacing smile. "I shouldn't have told you any of this darling. I'm sorry I did. You have your own problems. By the way, have you settled the question that was bothering you? I mean in your third chapter? I've been worrying about that all day," and on and on she went in this vein, the subject of her husband's unfaithfulness laid aside, as if she had put by her needlework for a more urgent activity.

I'll have to find out myself who the woman is, Dane decided. It's a cinch she'll never tell me, even if she knows. Probably took some typical Victorian vow against ever allowing her lips to be "sullied" by the creature's name.

"Never mind my third chapter, Mother. I'll say one thing more, and then I'll stop talking about this: Do you want to come live with me? Under the circumstances?" Even in broaching the possibility Dane felt like one of Nature's noblemen. The most rewarding act of his life so far had been to take an apartment of his own.

His mother looked at him. "Thank you, dear, but no."

"You're going to go on here with Father, as if nothing had happened?"

"I don't know what she is," Lutetia McKell said, "but I'm my husband's wife, and my place is with him. No, I'm not going to leave him. For one thing, it would make him unhappy . . ."

You, said Dane silently, are magnificence incarnate. You're also telling me a lie, which ladies do not do, or telling yourself one, which is far likelier, and more in accord with modern psychology. By God, the old girl had some iron in her after all! She was going to put up a fight.

Dane kissed her devotedly and left.

He had to find out who his father's mistress was.

Exactly why he must unveil the other woman, Dane did not pause to puzzle over, beyond wondering mildly at his compulsive need and overhastily discarding the notion that it had something to do with Freud.

It actually had to do with his mother. The mere thought of that pale and fragile creature setting out to do battle with the forces of cynicism aroused all his pity. It was an uneven fight. Somehow he had to find a way to help her. (And hurt his father? But to that point Dane did not go.)

He considered for only one horrid moment taking the direct route, confronting his father with his knowledge, demanding, "Who is she?" The whole scene was too embarrassing to contemplate. His father would either grasp him by the neck and the seat of the pants and hurl him bodily from the premises (and isn't the fear of physical punishment at those great father-hands deeply hidden inside you, Dane?) or, worse, he might break down and weep. Dane did not think he could stand either eventuality. (Or even a third possibility, which Dane did not consider: that his father might simply say, "It's none of your business, son," and change the subject.)

In any event, as Dane saw it, subterfuge was called for.

Ashton McKell's movements were generally predictable. He had fairly fixed times for getting to his office and coming home, for going to his club, for reading his newspaper, his magazines, his Complete Works of Rudyard Kipling. Home at seven, dinner at eight, five days a week. It was on weekends that the elder McKell did his personal brand of carousing; but at those times he caroused in the open.

Except . . .

Except, Dane suddenly realized, that for weeks now —or was it months?—his father had not got home until past his usual hour on one night of the week, Wednesday. Dane could not recall his mother's ever commenting on this phenomenon; and all that his father had said, on the single occasion when Dane brought the subject up, was the one word: "Business."

What "business" was it that recurred Wednesday nights regularly? It seemed an easy leap to the conclusion that on Wednesday nights Ashton McKell made rendezvous with his mistress.

Nothing could be done about it today, which was Tuesday. But tomorrow . . . His weekend plans would have to be scrapped, Dane told himself, nursing the hunch that it would be a busy time.

He turned to the mumble-sheet in his typewriter.

Jerry at the old stone quarry. Ellen comes, rest as noted. Okay, but. WHY does Jerry go there? To swim? April—too early. Maybe to fish. Check: fish in stone quarries?

He pulled at his lower lip. Then he cocked his head and his fingers raced over the keys.

The elder McKell left his office promptly at noon as marked on Taylor McKell's old Seth Thomas clock in the inner sanctum. Judy would quit her desk at 12:10, return at 12:55. Ashton would be back at 1 P.M. sharp,

August 17th, 12:05 P.M.:

"Judy? Dane McKell. My father there?"

"He's left, Dane. Is your watch slow?"

A rueful laugh. "Damn it, it is." Then, in a rush: "Look, Judy, I've got to see him this afternoon, but I can't make it till after five. Do you suppose—?"

"That's far too late, Dane. Today is Wednesday, and on Wednesdays Mr. McKell now leaves his office at four. Can't you make it before then?"

"Never mind, I'll catch him later, at home. Don't even bother mentioning my call. How are you, Judykins? But I'm keeping you from your lunch."

Judy thought as she hung up: That was an odd conversation. But then she shrugged and went off to lunch. She had long ago given up trying to figure out Dane McKell; too much thought about him was no good for her, anyway. The secretary married the boss's son only in the movies.

Out into the August sun went Dane. He rented a car, a two-year-old Ford. His own little red MG might be spotted.

He picked up the Ford at a quarter past three, and by 3:45 he was parked outside the McKell Building. He thought it unlikely that his father would sneak out through the boiler-room exit or one of the side doors. Sure enough, a few minutes later up drove the big Bentley with Ramon, his father's chauffeur, at the wheel.

Dane pulled away and circled the block. Now he parked at an observation post across the street, some distance behind the Bentley, and settled down to wait.

Ramon was reading a racing form.

What am I doing here? though Dane. What in God's name do I think I'm doing? Suppose I find out who the woman is, "unmask" her? Then what? How would that help Mother?

There was one possibility. Suppose the woman did not know her sugar-daddy was a married man. Suppose he had filled her full of a lot of hop about making an honest woman of her. One flea in her ear, and she might give him his hat.

And what does that make me? the McKell son and heir ruminated. A first-class heel is what!

Still . . . Dane shrugged. The compulsion was powerful. He had to find out the woman's name. He would take it—somewhere—from there.

At 4:10 he stiffened. The massive figure of his father came striding through the revolving doors of the McKell Building. Ramon dropped his racing form, jumped out, and held the rear door open. Ashton McKell got in, Ramon ran around to the front, started the Bentley, and the big car swished off into the traffic.

Rather frantically, Dane followed.

The Bentley headed for the West Side Highway. It went north past Washington Market, past the Old Sapolio Building, past the docks where the Atlantic liners berthed like comic-book monsters, Dane in the hired Ford keeping several lengths behind. Where were they going? Over the George Washington Bridge to some ghastly New Jersey suburb, where Ashton McKell was keeping the widow of some insurance salesman in bourgeois splendor? Or up to 72nd Street and a doxy's teddy-bear-filled flat?

But the Bentley turned off at a midtown exit, crept east over to Fifth Avenue, and headed north again. Dane had no opportunity to trim his speculations to the wind—he was too busy trying not to lose the other car.

Suddenly the chauffeur-driven car pulled up before a stout stone building of three stories which Dane knew well enough. He was puzzled. If there was one building in New York where his father could not possibly be holding an assignation, it was at this, the Metropolitan Cricket Club, that arch-bastion of ultra-respectable aristocrats.

Cricket itself no longer occupied the energies of the club, which had been founded in 1803 (Dane found himself thinking of Robert Benchley's *After 1903, What?*

—a good question). For who was left for the Metropolitan Cricketeers to play? The puberts of the Riverdale Country School? No British team would stoop to play them; and if the club membership could have brought themselves to step out onto a bowling pitch against the supple West Indian immigrants who still played cricket up in Van Cortlandt Park, the result would have been mayhem . . . It was a club, like other exclusive clubs, whose principal virtue was exclusivity. And indeed Dane gazed up at his elderly cousin twice removed, Colonel Adolphus Phillipse, who sat, seemingly growing out of the floor, in his window, with the *New York Times,* doubtless growling over the dangerous radicalism of Senator Barry Goldwater.

The Bentley drove off; Dane snapped around in time to see his father walking briskly up the worn front steps as if it were Tuesday or Friday, his club days. What was he going to do? Have a drink? Write a letter? Make a phone call? . . . Dane settled himself.

At the other side of the window, separated from Colonel Phillipse, sat white-whiskered Dr. Mac-Anderson, immersed in one of the bearded tomes from which for fifty years he had been culling information to support his theory that "the mixed multitude" which accompanied the children of Israel out of Egypt was in fact the ancestral horde of the Gypsy nation. Colonel Phillipse slowly turned a page of his newspaper, intent on not missing a semicolon of the latest transgression of the Federal Reserve Bank. And Dane wondered how long his father was going to remain inside.

He sat up quickly. The heat and the sluggard reveries of the two old men in the window had made him forget . . . *He's being very discreet,* his mother had said. *Taking special precautions.*

What if this stop at the club was a "special precaution"?

Dane hustled the rented Ford around the corner and —sure enough!—there, at the rear entrance of the club, outside a public garage, sat the empty Bentley—Ramon had disappeared, apparently dismissed—and just coming out was Dane's father.

Ashton McKell was no longer wearing the light linen suit made for him by Sarcy, his London tailor, nor the

21

shoes (fitted to his lasts) from Motherthwaite's, also of London, nor the hat of jipijapa fibers specially woven for him in Ecuador. The rather startling clothes he was now wearing Dane had never seen before. He also carried a walking stick and a small black leather satchel, like a medical bag.

Dane's brow wrinkled. These could hardly constitute "special precautions"—a mere change of clothing. What was he up to?

The elder McKell walked past the Bentley and without warning climbed into a black Continental limousine, took the wheel himself, and drove off.

The limousine turned north, east, south, west . . . Dane lost track of direction in his awkward efforts to keep the other car in sight. The Continental had old-fashioned curtained windows, like a hearse, and the curtains were now drawn. What the devil?

It poked its nose into Central Park and began describing parabolas, for what purpose Dane could not imagine. Not to throw off pursuers—it was going too slowly for that. Was he simply killing time?

Suddenly the limousine pulled up and stopped, and as Dane drove by he saw his father get out of the driver's seat and climb into the curtained rear. Dane parked around a nearby curve and waited with his engine running. He was baffled. Why had his father got into the rear of the car? There was no one else with him, Dane was almost positive. What could he be doing there?

Suddenly the Continental drove past him, heading toward an exit. Dane followed.

The limousine drove east and pulled up at a garage on a side street between Madison Avenue and Park. Dane slammed on his brakes, double-parking. He saw a garage mechanic come out with an orange ticket and reach into the Continental with it, nodding; he saw the driver of the Continental back out from behind the wheel and immediately hail a taxicab and jump in, to be driven off. The taxi had to stop at the corner of Park Avenue for a red light, and Dane pulled up directly behind it.

He was doubly puzzled now. There was something strange-looking about the passenger in the cab, viewed from the rear. But what it was he could not at the moment put his finger on.

The light changed, and the cab turned into Park Avenue. Dane turned, too . . . It was a very short trip, no more than six or eight blocks. The cab darted in toward the curb, its passenger jumped out, paid the driver, the cab drove off, and the passenger began to walk down Park Avenue.

Dane, creeping along, was utterly confused. His parents lived less than a block away. And the man who had got out of the taxi was not the same man who had driven the Continental away from the Cricket Club.

At least, that was Dane's first impression. The man had gray hair, rather long and untidy at the neck. He wore a gray mustache, a Vandyke beard, and eyeglasses. A stranger.

One hand grasped a walking stick, the other a small black leather bag. The man was dressed all in tan—tan cords, tan straw hat, tan shoes—the same costume, as far as Dan could remember, that his father had worn on emerging from the club. Had there been another man waiting in the Continental after all?—a man who had exchanged clothes with the elder McKell behind the drawn curtains when he had pulled up in Central Park?

But why? And who could he be?

And then Dane knew.

It was not a stranger. It was his father. Disregard the clothes, strip off the mustache, beard, and wig, and the pupa beneath was—had to be—Ashton McKell.

His father in a disguise! He had put on the make-up during the stop in Central Park, behind the drawn curtains.

Dane almost laughed aloud. But there was a pathetic quality about the figure walking stiffly along the street with cane and bag swinging that discouraged levity. What in the name of all that was unholy did he think he was doing? "Special precautions"! He looked like someone out of an old-time vaudeville act.

23

There was no place to park. Dane doubled-parked and took up the chase on foot. His face was grim.

It became grimmer.

For the disguised Ashton McKell turned neither right nor left. He stumped up to the entrance of a building and went in.

It was a converted old Park Avenue one-family mansion, originally owned by the haughty Huytenses. The last Huytens had left it to "my beloved pet and friend, Fluffy," but long before old Mrs. Huytens' cousins succeeded in having Fluffy legally disinherited, the house had begun to decline. Dane's maternal grandfather had made a bargain purchase of it in the later days of the depression and turned it into an apartment building. It housed three duplex apartments and a penthouse, and Dane knew it intimately.

He had been brought up in it.

It was his parents' home.

The pattern was now clear except for one point . . . the most important point.

Everything about his father's extraordinary precautions smacked of secrecy. The elder McKell on Wednesday afternoons had his chauffeur drive him in the Bentley to the Cricket Club. The Bentley was left in the garage behind the club, and Ramon, given a few hours off, discreetly vanished. Meanwhile Ashton McKell changed clothes in his room at the club. He sneaked out through the rear entrance, picked up the Continental, and drove away. In Central Park, at a secluded spot, he stopped the car, got into the rear of the tonneau, and applied his disguise. Then he drove over to a garage—he probably uses different ones, Dane thought—left the Continental, and took a taxi to the corner of the Park Avenue block where the McKell apartment building stood. And it was all so timed that he would enter the building while the doorman was at his dinner—a precaution against being recognized, in spite of the disguise, by John. He ran a lesser risk on leaving the building, when the doorman was back on duty, for John would not pay as much attention to a departing visitor as to an incoming one. The medical bag alone gave him some of the invisibility of Chesterton's postman.

And when he left, he simply went back to the garage where he had parked the Continental, drove down to the Cricket Club after removing his make-up—probably in Central Park again—changed back into his ordinary clothes in his room at the club, and had Ramon, back on duty, drive him home in the Bentley.

The unexplained question was: Whom was he doing all this for? Whom was he visiting in his own apartment building?

Dane waited for the tall gray-uniformed figure of the doorman to reappear under the canopy.

"Oh, Mr. Dane," the doorman said. "Mrs. McKell isn't in."

"Any notion where she went, John, or when she'll be back?"

"She went to that Mr. Cohen's gallery to see some rugs, she said." The doorman, as usual, transformed Mir Khan from Pakistani to a more comfortable New York name. "I don't know when she'll be back."

The doorman's "I don't know" sounded rather like *I dawn't knaw*. John Leslie was a "Geordie," or Tynesider, from the north of England; and his speech came out both Irish and Scottish, with rich overtones of South Carolina. In his teens Dane had smoked forbidden cigarets in Leslie's basement apartment, left and received messages there which presumably would have been frowned upon by his parents.

"Well," Dane said with deliberate indecisiveness. Then, with a laugh: "Incidentally, John, I noticed a man going into the building a while ago whom I'd never seen here before. While you were at dinner. Gray hair, chin whiskers, wearing glasses, and carrying a medical bag. Is somebody sick?"

"That would be Miss Grey's doctor," said John Leslie. "I saw him leave a few times and asked Miss Grey once who he was, and she said Dr. Stone. How are you coming along with your book, Mr. Dane? You must tell us when they print it, now. The missus and me have your other books, and we like them champion."

"Thanks, John." Dane knew that his two books lay in

25

the Leslies' cabinet beside their picture of the Royal Family. "Oh, don't mention to Mother that I've been by. She'd feel bad about missing me."

Dane made his way to Lexington Avenue and a bar that advertised *No Television*. The interior was cool and smelled of malt, as a proper bar should, and not of spaghetti sauce and meat balls, as a proper bar should not. He ordered a gin and tonic and drank it and ordered another.

Miss Grey. Sheila Grey.

She was "the other woman."

It was a proper shock.

Sheila Grey, rated on anyone's list, was among the Top Ten of international *haute couture*. And she was not much older than Dane (old enough, he thought, to be the old bull's daughter). In the United States her reputation as a fashion designer made her one of the Top Three; there were some who acclaimed her first among equals. She had the penthouse.

Dane reorganized his emotions. Whatever this was, it was no longer an ordinary liaison. Ash McKell certainly was not "keeping" Sheila Grey, who could well afford half a dozen penthouses; this could not be an affair of love-for-money. Could it be—he felt a chill—love? In that case, God help Mother!

And not the theatricalism made a little more sense. You couldn't meet a woman like Sheila Grey in a motel somewhere, or tuck her out of sight in the Westchester countryside. She would be strongly independent; as far as Dane knew, she was not married; if a lover were to rendezvous with her, it would have to be in her apartment. Since her apartment happened to be in the same building occupied by her lover and his wife, he could only visit her surreptitiously. Ash McKell had chosen disguise.

It must make him wriggle, Dane thought. His father's conservatism was constantly embattled with his zest for living; in this, as in other respects, he was a paradox. He would writhe at the necessity of making a fool of himself, at the same time that he mastered the technique of theatrical make-up. It was really rather skillfully done.

But then everything Ash McKell set out to do he did skillfully. Dane had never known that his father knew

26

karate until the night they caught a sneak thief in the McKell apartment. His father had broken the man's wrist and three of his ribs with no more than a few blurred gestures.

Dane ordered a third gin and tonic, and over this one he felt anger return. It was all very complex, no doubt, but there was nothing complex about Ashton McKell's romance. To commit adultery almost directly over his wife's head! It was plain vulgarity, mean as hell.

Did his mother know that her rival occupied the penthouse?

Dane tossed off his drink. Whether she knew or not (and if he were betting on it, he would have bet that she knew), something had to be done.

He did not attempt to rationalize the compulsion, any more than he could have rationalized his feelings toward his mother. She was silly, arbitrary, hopelessly old-fashioned, out of place and time, and he adored her. Whether he adored her because of what she was or in spite of it did not matter. Her reason for being was threatened, and who else was there to remove the threat?

Now a rather leering interloper crept into his thoughts.

What to do next . . . break up the affair, certainly, but how? He asked the question, not rhetorically—he had no doubt that it could be done—but in order to organize his *modus operandi* . . . That was when the intruder crept in.

For the first time, under the liberating influence of the alcohol, Dane admitted to himself that his feelings were not unmixed. He did feel sorry for his mother. He did feel angry with his father. But why was he also feeling enjoyment? Self-satisfaction, really?

Dane ordered another gin and tonic.

First, there had been the ridiculous ease with which he had uncovered the identity of his father's paramour, and their trysting place. Small as the triumph was, it gratified him. We all like to think we're so noble, he reflected, when what really pleases us in our relationships with others is *our* little part in events, not theirs.

To self-satisfaction he had to add excitement. The emotion was definitely there, his personal response to a challenge. It derived from the nature of the situation. It was a story situation—one of the oldest in literature,

27

true; still, it might have come from anyone's typewriter. It raised plot questions. How would I handle it if it were a situation in one of my stories? Could people be manipulated in life as handily as on paper? If they could . . . Here was real creation!—the creation of action and re-action in context with a cast of flesh-and-blood characters, one of whom was himself.

And the delicious, the best part of it was that it would be done without any of the principals being in the least aware that they were puppets!

Am I a monster? Dane wondered, sipping moodily at his fourth gin and tonic. But then aren't all writers monsters? Cannibals feeding off the flesh of friends and enemies alike, converting them into a different form of energy for the sheer joy of digestion? (And how much of it, Dane thought ruefully, followed the human econo-my and went down the drain!) The truth was, any writ-er worth his salt would give a year off his life for a chance like this. (Thackeray coming downstairs, weep-ing. "What is the matter, Henry?" "I have just killed Colonel Newcombe!" How the old boy would have ris-en, like a trout to the lure, to such an opportunity!) It was commonplace for authors to make lemonade out of the lemons handed them by life, and poor pink stuff it became, too. How would the real thing look and taste . . . ?

By the sixth gin Dane was drawing bold lines on the table with the condensation from his glass. Thus, thus, and thus:

He would contrive to meet Sheila Grey.

He would make love to her.

He would make her love him.

He would displace his father in her life.

That should do it.

How would his father react to being deposed by his son? Or by having to "share the latchkey" with him (Dane's writing mind foresaw the possibility that this Sheila, still uncomprehended, might be the sort of wom-an to whom the notion of sleeping with father and son on alternate nights was amusing)? Of course, he felt sor-ry for the old man (how old is old, Dane?). The blow to his ego would be shattering. Well, serve him right. Send him back where he belongs, to Mother.

After that, what? Drop her, go back to work? Why not? Serve *her* right, breaking up a solid 'Murrican home, Episcopal yet! Dane chuckled, the chuckle turning giggly.

There was no doubt in his mind, after the seventh gin and tonic, that he could pull it off. What the deuce 'd she look like? He tried vainly to recall. He had passed her in the lobby on three or four occasions, but each encounter had happened to coincide with a love affair, when other women hardly existed for him. He had seen her photo in *Vogue* and the Sunday papers several times, but her face remained a blank. She couldn't be outstandingly ugly, or some impression would have lingered. So she must be relatively pleasant to look at, thank heaven.

He decided to order just one more drink.

He was hung over when the telephone rang on his desk. The shrilling made him wince. It was all of a piece with his general outlook on life this morning, for his cogitations had led him into a cul-de-sac, and he had not yet worked his way out of it.

In sober determination to act boldly, he had composed imaginary dialogue for their opening conversation:

Miss Grey, I'm working on another novel—I don't know if you've seen my earlier ones . . . ?

I'm afraid not, Mr.Kell, although I've heard about them. (That seemed a reasonable preconstruction. The elder McKell could hardly have avoided mentioning his son's literary achievements, such as they were, and Sheila Grey, a VIP in her own right, could hardly be construed as caring a damn.)

My books haven't raise anything yet but a slight stench, I'm afraid. But I have high hopes for this one—if you'll help me.

If I'll help you, Mr. McKell? (That would be the raised-eyebrow department. Perhaps a shade interested.)

You see, Miss Grey, one of my leading characters is that of a famous dress designer. If I wanted to research

29

a cab driver, all I'd have to do is ride around in cabs. But a great fashion figure—I'm afraid you're the only accessible one I've heard of. Or am I presuming?

Ordinarily what she would say was *You certainly are,* but under the circumstances he foresaw a *Well . . . just how can I help you?*

The secret of making people interested in you, Dane had learned, lay not in helping them but in getting them to help you. *By letting me watch you at work* would be the irresistible response. She was bound, no matter how jaded fame had made her, to be flattered.

Or was she?

Here was where Dane's hangover had ached.

Sheila Grey might be flattered if he were Tom Brown or Harry Schnitzelbach. But he was Ashton McKell's son. His head throbbed with caution. To achieve an appointment he would have to give her his name. And no matter how little time elapsed between his request for an appointment and his plea for her help, it would be more than long enough to set her to wondering.

And to becoming forewarned and, therefore, forearmed.

It wouldn't do.

So he had been prowling his apartment, chewing on his thoughts, trying to crack the problem. *If you can't go through, go around* kept running about in his head. But he could not think of how to go around.

That was when the telephone rang, and he winced and answered it.

It was Sarah Vernier.

"You're annoyed, Dane," she said. "I can tell. I've interrupted your work."

"No, Aunt Sarah, it's just that—"

"Dear, I simply wanted to know if you'd come up to Twenty Deer for the weekend."

Mrs. Vernier was not his aunt, she was his godmother; and it was not spiritual consanguinity that drew them together but a mutual fondness of long standing. Twenty Deer had been one of his favorite places as a boy; and

30

Sarah Vernier's charm, plus the excellence of her table and her French husband's cellar, preserved its attractions for him as an adult. It was the estate near Rhinebeck which—before his mother's revelation—had been one of his possible choices for the weekend he had sworn not to spend in the city.

"I'm afraid it's impossible, Aunt Sarah," Dane said.

"Shoot!" she said. "What is it with everyone? Somebody must be spreading the rumor that we have the plague up here."

"I wish I could come, I really do."

"I'll bet you do. It's a new girl, isn't it, you devil?" Mrs. Vernier sounded pleased. "Tell me about her."

"It's worse. A new book, Aunt Sarah."

"Oh, dear, that obsession of yours." The weekend was ruined, no one was coming to Twenty Deer, she would be alone with Jacques—sweet man, wasn't he? but one of those infernal enthusiasts. Two years ago it was organic farming, last year orchids, now it's falcons.

"Messy, smelly, savage things," said Mrs. Vernier. "Fortunately, he keeps them in the barn, so I'm spared the sight of them. As a result, of course, I never see Jacques, either. I've half a mind to come into town, just to teach him a lesson."

And, "Why don't you?" said Dane strongly.

It was as easy as that. In a moment he would be astonished at the speed of his inspiration; now he had time for nothing but following it up.

"But everyone's away, dear," Sarah Vernier said. "No one at all is left in New York."

"You can always," Dane said, "do some shopping."

"But with whom? You're aware, my dear, that your mother is no fun, bless her—she might as well get her things from the Salvation Army. And you're too busy. Or," she asked suddenly, "are you?"

"For you, Aunt Sarah? Never!"

So easy. Sarah Vernier and her shopping were proverbial in and about their circle. It was one of the few subjects on which she could be a bore. So Dane knew all about her favorite shopping places.

As usual, she began with trivia and worked her way up. She visited Tiffany's and ordered—for her husband—cuff links with falcons on them. Then she picked up two cut-glass toothpick holders at the Carriage House for her collection. At a "new little place" in the East 80s she (eventually) came away with a "darling" hat. At Leo Ottmiller's bookshop, since the falcon-ridden Jacques's happiness was still on her conscience, Mrs. Vernier purchased *The Boke of the Hawke*.

They lunched at the Colony.

She attacked her vichyssoise and cold chicken with good appetite. "Where shall we go next?" she asked. "Oh, Dane, this *was* an inspiration. I'm having such fun!"

"Macy's?"

"Don't be *wicked*. I know!" she cried. "Sheila Grey's."

And Dane said—as if he had not brought Sarah Vernier half the length of the Hudson Valley for this sole purpose without her slightest suspicion of it—"Sheila Grey's? Of course," with just the right touch of vagueness. He must have heard her say it a hundred times: *I always get my things at Sheila Grey's.*

On the sidewalk outside the Colony, she said, "You look like a porter on safari. Why don't we leave the packages somewhere?"

"They're light as air." It was an important part of his plan to arrive at his goal looking the very picture of Gentleman Helping Lady on Extended Shopping Tour. He handed her into the taxicab before she could insist.

So here they were.

Sheila Grey's Fifth Avenue salon.

While Mrs. Vernier was exchanging greetings with the sharply tailored, gray-haired chief of saleswomen, Dane artfully wandered off, still holding his godmother's packages. He did not want to set them down. Not just yet.

He had become genuinely interested in the reproduction of a Pieter de Hooch—whoever selected the pictures in the salon had evidently not learned his trade at the feet of those who decorated American hotel rooms with thousands of mock-Utrillos and psuedo-Georgia

32

O'Keefes—when a voice behind him said, "Let me take those from you, Mr. McKell."

Wheeling, he looked into the face of a woman his own age, chic, a little abstracted, the tidiest bit untidy. Dane was about to decline when she simply took the packages from him.

"My name is Sheila Grey, Mr. McKell."

It could not have been more beautifully executed if he had prepared two weeks for this moment. He had not seen her approach, he had not recognized her, and his reaction was therefore genuine.

"Thanks, Miss Grey. How stupid of me not to recognize you."

She handed the packages to a young woman who had materialized from somewhere and just as promptly snuffed herself out; and she smiled.

"There's no reason why you should. If you were a female, I'd be worried."

Dane murmured something.

His heart had not jumped; his flesh was not crawling; he was feeling neither rage nor contempt. He was wondering why when Sarah Vernier came up, beaming. "Sheila, this is my godson, Dane McKell. Isn't he lovely?"

"I'd hardly select that adjective, Mrs. Vernier," Sheila Grey smiled. "Or don't you object to it, Mr. McKell?"

"I never object to anything Aunt Sarah says, Miss Grey. Incidentally, how did you know who I am?"

"I beg your pardon?"

"You addressed me by name twice a few moments ago."

"Did I?" Did her make-up conceal the slightest flush? "I suppose I must have known who you were from seeing you in the lobby of your parents' apartment building. You know I have the penthouse?"

"Of course," said Dane ruefully. "This is my stupid day."

She was neither short nor tall. She was slender, on the pale side (or was that her make-up?), with lustrous brown hair and gray, gray eyes. Her features were so regular that they seemed to Dane to have no character; certainly he would never have invented her as a *femme fatale* for a book. He wondered what had attracted his father, who had access—if he wanted to take advantage of his opportunities—to scores of far more beautiful women. It was not her youth alone; youth could be bought, or rented. There had to be something special about her; and he felt a slight anticipation.

"Is this part of the international *couturière's* image?" Dane asked, gazing around. "I mean all this unoccupied space? Or do you have invisible customers, Miss Grey?"

"They're invisible at this time of the year." She smiled back. "The summer doldrums are at their height. Or is it depth? However you measure doldrums."

"I'm not enough of a sea-dog to know."

"Dane, I thought writers knew *everything*," said Sarah Vernier, delighted at the opening thus presented to her. "You know, Sheila, Dane's in town working on his new *book*."

"Then you and I are in the same leaky boat, Mr. McKell." Her eyebrows (unplucked, he noticed) had gone up.

"You're writing a book, too? On *haute couture*, I suppose."

"Heavens, I can barely write my name." He rather liked her laugh; it was fresh and brisk and brief, like a frank handshake. "No, I'm staying in town to work on my new collection." Sarah Vernier went, "Ohhhhhh . . . !" with a rising inflection. The showing was scheduled for November, the designer went on. "I should really be home at my drawing board right now. In fact . . ." Dane saw that she was preparing gracefully to withdraw.

"Sheila, you mustn't!" wailed Mrs. Vernier. After all, she had come all the way from Rhinebeck, no one else could wait on her properly, she wanted summer and fall things, too—"Dane, *help* me."

"I'd be the last one to keep another suffering soul from creative agony, Miss Grey, but if you'll spare Aunt Sarah a little more of your time I'll drive you home afterward."

And "There!" exclaimed Mrs. Vernier in a you-can't-refuse-now tone of voice. And "Oh, no, no, that won't be necessary—" Sheila, hurriedly. *And how do you like the pressure, dear heart . . . ?* Dane went on

34

boyishly: He had never met a designer before, he threw himself on her fellow craftsmanship, and so on. "And think of poor Aunt Sarah, doomed to wear the same miserable rags."

"I'll have you know, Mr. McKell, those 'rags' came from my shop."

"Oh, but Sheila," cried Mrs. Vernier, "I got them here in April."

"The riposte supreme," Dane murmured. "Surely you can't expect a woman to wear clothes she bought in April? It's unconstitutional, Miss Grey."

"Is that a sample of your dialogue?" Sheila dimpled "Well, all right. But if the French and Italians sweep ahead of us next season, you'll know just where the fault lies."

"I accept the awesome responsibility. I'll turn myself over for being spat upon and stoned."

"While I go bankrupt. Now, Mr. McKell, you sit over there on that chesterfield and twiddle your thumbs. This is women's work."

It was clear that she was, if not exactly interested, at least amused. Perhaps, too, the element of danger contributed to her decision. Or am I overstating the situation? Dane thought. Maybe she figures this is the easiest way to get rid of me. Give the little boy what he wants and then send him off with Auntie.

"Sheila, what do you think about this one?"

"I don't. Billie, take that away. Bring the blue and white shantung." After a while, skillfully, the designer had Sarah Vernier almost entirely in the charge of her staff, while she sat beside Dane and they chatted about books and New York in midsummer and a dozen other things. Occasionally she put in a word to resolve a doubt of Mrs. Vernier's, or overrule a suggestion of her salespeople. It was all most adroitly done. She can handle people, Dane thought. I wonder just how she goes about handling Dad.

"I think we've crossed the Rubicon," Sheila Grey said suddenly, rising. Dane jumped up. "Mrs. Vernier won't have to wear rags after all. Now I really must get home." home."

"I'll drive you, as promised."

"You'll do nothing of the sort, Mr. McKell, although

it's noble of you to make the offer. You have to take care of Mrs. Vernier. I'll grab a taxi."

"Supper?" he asked quickly.

She looked at him—almost, he thought, for the first time. Had he pulled a boner? Going too fast? She had remarkable directness in her cool gray eyes that warned him to be very cautious indeed.

"Why would you want to take me to supper, Mr. McKell?"

"I have ulterior motives. The fact is, I have to research a designer—and I can't think of a pleasanter way to do it, by the way, now that I've met the woman Aunt Sarah's raved about so long. Is it a date?"

"It is not. I'm going home and working right through the weekend."

"I'm sorry. I've made a bloody pest of myself."

"Not at all. It's I who's sounding ungracious. I could lunch with you on Monday."

"Would you? That's awfully kind. One-ish? One-thirty? Name the time and place, Miss Grey."

Sheila hesitated. It seemed to Dane that she found herself in a dilemma. That means I'm not repulsive to her, he thought; and he felt a tingle suddenly.

"If you're really interested in my work, in the whole area of fashion . . . Tell you what, Mr. McKell. Why don't you plan to get here a bit earlier Monday? Say, at noon? Then we can go over some of the basic things."

"Wonderful," said Dane. "You can't know what this means to me, Miss Grey. Monday at noon, then. Aunt Sarah?"

"Oh, you two *do* like each other," cried Mrs. Vernier, glowing.

Dane had been normally aware that women wore clothes and that their creation was a matter of considerably more moment than, say, the designing of a nuclear flattop. He knew vaguely that there was rivalry between the Continental and American dress houses, and that it resulted in a secrecy that made the answer to *Does Macy's tell Gimbel's?* meekly affirmative. But he was hardly prepared to find Pinkerton guards standing watch over every nook and cranny of Sheila Grey's establishment except the salon itself.

"It's almost like the CIA!" he exclaimed.

The comparison was not inexact. In a hugely different degree, on an infinitely smaller scale, the behind-the-scenes scenes of high fashion did have a faint air of the Pentagon gone mad. Men with the dedicated look of the career idealist, women who gave the impression of having studied at the secretive feet of Mata Hari, zealous underlings of the three sexes, and assorted females who could have been camp followers, sat poring over plans, screwed up their tired eyes at sketches, moved from office to office in zombie-like withdrawal; they examined swatches as if the bits of material were secret weapons, and peered with tucked-in lips at lovely young models who, for all the excitement their beauty generated, might have been made of plastic. Here clothes were the only living things.

"And this is an annual event?" Dane asked.

"Yes. Let me show you." Dane followed Sheila, attending her litany—Marc Bohan of Dior, Crahay of Nina Ricci, Castillo of Lanvin (like so many medieval saints, or feudatories, or even Isaac of York or Macdonald of the Isles), Cardin, Chanel, Jacques Heim, Balmain, Goma, Vernet, and the all but hallowed Yves St. Laurent. From Sheila's tone, Dane gathered that St. Laurent could cure scrofula by a laying on of hands.

"And that's just France," Sheila was saying.

He was actually taking notes.

"It's like wine," Sheila explained. "Any reasonable Frenchman will admit that certain French wines are inferior to their American counterparts. But we're such snobs! We'd rather tipple a mediocre vintage with a French label than a first-rate California. It's the same with clothes. All right, St. Laurent is tops. But it's not because he's French, it's because he's St. Laurent. Another thing that blows me sky-high is the women who won't wear a gown unless it's designed by a man. It makes me want to spit!"

"It becomes you," said Dane. It did, too; anger put color into her cheeks, and a sparkle in her eyes that made them flash.

She stopped herself with one of her fresh, quick laughs. "Let's go to lunch."

"I had forgotten lunch could be fun," Sheila Grey said. "Thank you, Mr. McKell."

"Could you make it Dane?"

"Dane. Are you sure you're writing a book with a designer-character in it?"

"Why would you doubt it?"

"I suppose I don't care for people with hidden motives." She laughed. "I'm always on the watch."

"The only hidden motive I could have would be *very* personal, and I can't imagine any woman resenting that."

"At this point," said Sheila, rising, "I've got to get back to the galleys."

"Can we do this again soon? Tomorrow?"

"I shouldn't . . ."

"Another session at your place, then lunch again?"

"Get thee behind me! All right, I surrender," and that was that. He took her back to Fifth Avenue, and she talked shop all the way, Dane scribbling away.

Taking stock of the afternoon, he came to certain conclusions about Sheila Grey. She was accessible, at least in the sense that what Sheila fancied, Sheila took. Had her affair with his father begun in much the same way—directly, without persiflage? Had she run into Ashton McKell in the elevator, decided then and there, *This man is for me,* and invited him up for a drink?

He found himself wishing that he were meeting her under other circumstances. He admired her honesty of mind and manner, her forthright differences from most women—even the sprinkle of freckles he had faintly made out in natural light. Oddly, she did not arouse a man's fighting instinct in the battle of the sexes. You could move comfortably in on her, without fuss, and she would either reject or accept in an uncomplicated way. He liked that.

Dane sighed. Between himself and Sheila Grey stood his father's selfish arrogance and his mother's helpless

38

self-denial. This woman had chosen to become his father's mistress a couple of dozen feet above the head of his mother; she would have to take the consequences.

But the only sinister thing in their growing relationship skulked in his own heart. Sheila was delightful. She chewed popcorn like teenagers around them in a drive-in movie, watching a Blob from Outer Space crush tiny people underfoot and topple buildings until the clean-limbed young scientist with the gorgeous laboratory assistant destroyed him with his newly invented death ray. She clapped her hands at a tiny place he introduced her to, run by devotees of a Hindu sect, and ate her curds and whey as if she had stepped out of a Mother Goose book. When the bearded proprietor pressed a piece of fig candy on her, saying, "It promotes regularity, *Sahibah*," Sheila smiled, and took it, and remarked, "I wish something could be done to promote regularity in high fashion. We caught someone using a miniature camera this morning. Naturally I fired him and destroyed the film. But you can't help wondering if somebody got away with it yesterday. We'll know about it if copies of our line go on sale on 14th Street, selling for $7.98, the day after our fall showing."

It appeared that the art of *couture* espionage was highly developed. "I could give you material for a dozen novels," Sheila said moodily.

"I'm having enough trouble with this one," Dane said, grinning. "Incidentally, how about dinner at eight?"

This time her gaze impaled him. "You're silly," she said. "Nice, though. I'll be wearing a mantilla and chewing on a red, red rose."

Dane began to feel uneasy. Things were going too well. But then he shook the feeling off.

They dined at a little Belgian restaurant with outrageous prices, took a ferry ride to Staten Island, visited Hoboken, where they strolled about for a bit, agreeing that parts of the city had a Continental air—Dane compared it to the 14th Arondissement. On the ferry coming back, standing side by side in the bow, he took Sheila's hand. She might have been any woman he liked. Her fingers lay cool and friendly in his clasp; the breeze lifted her hair and played with it. The great docks loomed, and Dane felt a twinge. Quite without calculation he said, "How about the Central Park Zoo tomorrow? The grilled armadillo there is out of this world."

"You'd produce it, too." Sheila's laugh sounded wistful. "No, Dane, I've been playing hooky far too long. You're wicked-bad for me."

"Supper? I know an Armenian joint—"

"I really can't, I'm too far behind. Tomorrow is out."

Tomorrow was Wednesday. The thought struck him like a club. Of course. She wouldn't date Yves St. Laurent himself on a Wednesday night. Wednesday nights were reserved for Daddy-o.

But there were other days and nights—the fights, the ballet, opera in a Connecticut barn, a county fair, a formal dinner at Pavillon one night and chopped liver at Lindy's the next. On several occasions they spent the evening at Sheila's apartment, listening to the hi-fi or viewing the summer re-runs on TV. On such occasions Sheila fed him.

"I have an understanding with the frozen-food people," she told Dane, paraphrasing the old joke. "They don't design clothes and I don't stand over a hot cookbook."

"Don't apologize," Dane said. "TV dinners constitute our only native art-form."

She laughed, throwing her head back. Viewing the cream-smooth neck, he felt a lecherous stir and wondered if he shouldn't encourage it. After all, he had been squiring her around for some time now without a single pass. Wouldn't she begin to wonder?

The phone rang. Still laughing, Sheila answered it. "Oh, hi," she said, in a remarkably different tone, moving back into the chair; and Dane sighed—the moment had gone. "How are you? . . . No, I'm fine . . . I couldn't say." She glanced at Dane, a mere flicker, and he said to himself: It's my father. He got up and went to

40

the window, and her voice sank. The reflection showed him a scowling and—it seemed to him—evil face.

"I'd like a drink," Sheila said from behind him. The phone call was over; comedy, recommence! "Something tall and ginny. Be my bartender?"

He turned to her; they were face to—the image persisted, it seemed to him—evil face. She seemed faded, even coarse, the smile on her lips complacent. *This is the way of an adulterous woman,/ She eateth and wipeth her mouth and sayeth,/ I have done no wrong* . . . He felt sick at heart, and he was glad of the excuse to turn away and tinker with bottles and ice cubes.

From time to time Sheila received other telephone calls—twice in her office while he was with her, twice more in her apartment—which, he assumed from her guarded tone, were also from his father.

One night at the end of August they attended an old movie in an art theater on the Lower East Side; it was almost 3 A.M. when they emerged. In the car he put his arm around her. She slipped away. "I don't believe in one-arm driving. Isn't this safer?" She put her arm around him.

In spite of himself, Dane felt a shiver. "Shall we stop somewhere? How about Ratner's and a glass of borsht?"

"That pink soup with sour cream in it?" Sheila pursed her lips. "I think I'd prefer a nightcap. Let's have it at my place."

"All right."

It seemed natural. Entering the apartment building lobby was, as always when he was in Sheila's company, something of a shock—knowing that his parents lay asleep overhead—but he had steeled himself by this time; he did not dwell on it. He did not dwell on much of anything these days.

"Come in, Dane."

"I'm suddenly reminded," Dane said, following Sheila into the penthouse apartment, "of the experience of a friend of mine. He accepted the offer of a tropical-looking beauty he met at a party to come up and have a

41

nightcap in her apartment, and when they walked in, lo, there pacing the floor was an economy-size ocelot. Arthur swears it was as big as a leopard. Needless to say, all he got that night was a drink, and he spilled half of that on the rug."

"Well, my ocelot got the evening off," Sheila said, "so don't spill yours. Not on this rug. Handwoven in Jutland, I'll have you know. Name your poison, pardner."

The living room, furnished in Scandinavian Modern, was dimly lighted. Always peaceful-looking, it seemed extraordinarily so on this occasion. A feeling of contentment invaded Dane, in the van of which marched a wiry little excitement. It was the queerest thing. Sheila mixed their drinks at her bar, humming to herself the absurd tune to an absurd W. C. Fields song they had heard at the art movies; she reached for the ice, and he caught a quiet smile on her face.

So it happened—not by calculation, not with his father standing aghast and outraged in the living-room archway, not as part of a created plot, but as naturally as breathing. Dane put his arms around her. Sheila turned with the same smile, lifted her perfect face and half closed her eyes, and they kissed.

Her lips, her body, were sweet and soft and full. He had never thought of her body before except in a repellent image, lying in his father's hairy arms.

Dane heard her say, "I'm glad you waited, darling," saw her hand him his drink, raise her own. They drank in silence, looking into each other's eyes. Then Dane set his glass down and took her hand, her strong white little hand with the smudge of violet india ink on the palm, and he kissed it, a brush of his lips; and left.

As he dressed for bed, the thought occurred to him for the first time that night: *I've accomplished my purpose. I've got her. Now all I have to do is arrange the pay-off.*

But it's gone all to pot.

And the horrifying thought: *I've fallen in love with her.*

He was in love with his father's mistress. It was not as if the kiss symbolized a beginning; it was an ending, a climax of days and nights of exploration and intermingling of ideas and attitudes and laughter and close silences; a seal to a compact they—he—had never suspected they were making. *I'm glad you waited, darling . . .* It was the same with her; she had experienced the special quality of their relationship, sealed with the kiss. If there was a beginning at all, it was not the beginning of an affair; it was the beginning of a lifetime.

Suddenly the whole incredible structure crashed about his head. Whom was he punishing? His father, yes; but his mother more. Himself most of all.

It was not supposed to be that way. It was all wrong, twisted out of any semblance to the shape he had been fashioning. Everyone was going to be hurt—mother, father, himself . . . and Sheila.

He tossed for most of what was left of the night.

Dane awakened to a sense of purpose, almost recklessness. That was the way it had worked out. The hell with everything else.

But with breakfast came caution. Think it over, he told himself, don't rush it, perhaps you're reading a fantasy into what could have been a mere kiss of the moment, as meaningless to you as to Sheila. He did not really feel that way, and he was sure that Sheila did not; still, it had to be taken into account. Take a day or so to simmer down, to let matters adjust themselves to some realistic yardstick.

As the day wore on he found himself hungering for her voice. Work was out of the question. Suppose by his silence he made her think he was having second thoughts? She mustn't think that, mustn't. Besides . . . that voice, that deep and husky telephone quality it did not have at other times . . .

"Sheila! Dane."

"I know."

It was like warm honey, that voice.

"I've got to see you. Tonight? This afternoon?"

"No, Dane, I want to think."

"Tomorrow?"

"Yes."

"I love you, Sheila."

She did not reply at once, as if she were fighting him, or herself. "I know, Dane," she finally said. "Tomorrow."

She came straight into his arms. There was a nerve in the hollow of her throat that jumped when he kissed it. It was sometime before he said anything. Then he held her close and said, "Sheila, I want you to marry me."

"I know, Dane."

She knew!

"Then you will?" he cried.

"No."

It was like setting his foot down where a step should have been, but was not. A scalding wave of humiliation washed over him; and suddenly he thought of his father. This was how his father would feel; this was his punishment for having planned the whole dirty thing. Was she laughing at him? Had she seen through him from the start?

He looked at her wildly.

"Darling, I'm not refusing you," murmured Sheila, and she took his head between her hands and kissed him on the lips.

"I guess I'm too thick-witted to get it."

"I love you, Dane. You can have me right now. But not as your wife."

Not as my wife? "Are you married?" *She was married . . .*

"Heavens, no!" She laughed at that. Then she looked into his face and without a word went to the bar and splashed brandy into a snifter and held the glass to his lips. He took it from her roughly.

"You mean you'll sleep with me," he said, "but you won't marry me."

"That's right, darling."

"But you just said you love me."

"I do."

"Then I don't understand!"

She stroked his cheek. "I suppose you considered yourself a thoroughly seasoned old rip, and here you have to discover that you're just a sweet old square. No, not yet, Dane. I must get this over to you. It's important to both of us."

What she went on to say was not at all what he was expecting. She made no reference to Ashton McKell; she was not, after all, rejecting a new love in favor of the incumbent. She had known for some time, she told Dane, tht she loved him.

"I'm speaking only for myself, dearest—I know my ideas are anti-social, and that society couldn't exist if everyone acted according to my views. I'm essentially a selfish woman, Dane. It's not that I don't care about what happens to people; but I'm most concerned with what happens to me in this very short life we're given. I suppose I'm a materialist. My notion of love doesn't require marriage to consummate it, that's all. In fact—I'm speaking only for myself—I reject the whole concept of marriage. I'm no more capable of being happy as a housewife, or a country club gal, or a young suburban matron than I am of renouncing the world and taking the veil.

"Maybe love and marriage go together like a horse and carriage, as the song says," Sheila went on, taking his cold hand, "but I'm an electronic-age-type dame. To me a ring on the finger is like a ring in the nose. What a mockery modern marriage is! No wonder divorce is one of our leading industries. I can't stomach the hypocrisy of marriage, so I side-step it. Can you picture me billing and cooing ten years after in a vine-covered cottage beside a waterfall?"

She laughed. He looked at her woodenly.

"The trouble is, of course, that I don't need a man to support me. I certainly don't need your money—I have plenty of my own. I don't hanker after social position; I have a pretty elevated position in my own sector of society. And I certainly couldn't subordinate myself to your career, because I have my own—what's worse, mine is made, while yours is still in the making. Marriage is all right for women in a bourgeois society . . ."

"What about children?" Dane asked her bitterly. "Doesn't your advanced concept include the little matter of children?"

"Not especially. Let those propagate the race who can't propagate anything else; Lord knows there are enough of them. I love children as much as the next woman, but in this life we have to make hard choices. I've made mine, and motherhood has no place in it. So you see, Dane, what you've fallen in love with."

"I see, yes," he said.

"We can be happy without marriage. As long as we stay in love. Don't you see that, darling?"

It seemed to him there was anxiety in her eyes. As for him, the Grand Marnier was gone by now, together with his anger and most of his sickness. Only emptiness was left.

"No, Sheila, I don't. I don't say what you propose is immoral—the hell with that; it's worse. It's impractical. If marriage without love is hateful, so is love without marriage. It has to creep instead of walk, skulk in dark corners, hide—"

"It has to do no such thing," Sheila retorted. Her head was cocked, her tone cool. "You're talking like a schoolboy, darling, do you know that? Last night—satisfied with a kiss in the dark. Really, Dane! And now this goody-goody talk. What's next? Are you going to tell me you've been keeping yourself chaste for your one and only little wifie? The difference between us is that you're a romantic, and I'm a merchant realist."

So there it was—the shrew hidden in every woman, the flash of carnivorous teeth, the bite.

He had thought of himself as taking his pleasure when and where he could create it, a reasonably sophisticated man. And here was Sheila, making him feel like a—what had she called him?—a schoolboy! Looking at her, he felt abjectly estranged. No trace of warmth or womanliness seemed left in the symmetrical face before him. It was like a Greek sculpture, smoothly inscrutable with secrets buried in time. Her philosophy was as far beyond him as his was beyond his mother's. Maybe he was still a Yaley at heart: have fun while you're unattached, then settle down with a wife—have fun afterward, too, if you could get away with it.

But Sheila's philosophy seemed contemptuous of any standard. He was sure he could never catch up with her, even surer that he didn't want to. And yet . . . a line from a poem he had jeered at came into his head: *La Belle Dame sans Merci/Hath thee in thrall.*

It was as if she knew it, for she chuckled; and even this tiny sound from her throat made him hunger.

46

"Oh, Dane, don't look so woebegone," she cried. "Instead of being married lovers, we'll be lovers, period. Dane . . . don't tell me you've never had a woman!" She looked at him with absolute horror.

He was glad that she was not smiling when she said it, or he might have leaped at her. The brandy had been a mere stopgap; the beginning of the old feared roaring stirred in his ears. Careful, he warned himself; keep control, as he felt his hands become fists.

"Yes, I've had women, but I must seem impossibly old-fashioned to you. Because I'm strictly a one-woman man. Well, I've had my share of disappointments. This seems to be another of them."

"Oh, Dane." She moved away a little. "You say you're a one-woman man. Don't you mean you're a one-woman-at-a-time man? And that's just right with me. I shouldn't want it any other way. I've no intention of sharing you with somebody. We're not far apart at all. Isn't that true?" When his mouth clamped tighter, Sheila said, "I don't mean I'd never consider marriage. In a way, it would be up to you to show me that marriage—with you—is what I really want.

"But I don't want it at this particular time, not even with you. I'm a one-man-at-a-time gal, and right now that man can be you. But you must understand that while I'd be yours and yours only, I don't know for how long. A week, a month, five years—maybe forever; how can either of us tell? You notify me when you want out, and I'll do the same."

Was he, could he really be, in love with her?

Dane began to pace, and Sheila sat back and watched him with that same trace of anxiety. Did this mean she was giving the old man the gate? Or was she playing some sort of game with both of them? Damn this development! It had really fouled everything up. (How could love foul up anything? So maybe he wasn't in love with her after all.)

He stopped before the ottoman and took her hands in his.

"All right, baby, we'll let the plot write itself. On your terms. Maybe I've escaped a fate worse than death. Lovers, is it? Let's get started."

Her arms tugged, and he let himself fall.

The next morning he was in a more comfortable frame of mind. Having savored the taste and depths of her, he could not doubt her. It was not a game—however brief it might turn out to be, it was not a game. He was convinced that she had told him the truth.

So Sheila was a one-man-at-a-time woman, and he had accomplished his purpose. In her forthrightness, Sheila would certainly have told his father, at the start of their affair, what she had told Dane; so it could come as no surprise to him when she broke it off.

This should send his father back to his mother, with no need for a confrontation—no need, when it came to that, for either of his parents to know how the trick had been accomplished. There was no reason for the elder McKell to learn that Sheila's new lover was his son; and let Lutetia think her husband had settled back in the nest of his own volition. It could comfort her.

But something was—not exactly wrong; off-key, perhaps. He offered Sheila a key to his apartment, and she refused it. "Not yet, darling. I'm still enjoying my illicit status." Instead, she offered him a key to hers.

And when the following Wednesday came, he could not see her. "I'm only human, darling," she said over the phone, a smile in her voice. "Not tonight. Tomorrow night?"

That Wednesday night, as usual, Ashton McKell did not come home at his other-weekday hour. He was gone all evening.

Sheila had lied to him. It must be that. Yet how could it be? Or was she easing his father off? That was it. He was probably taking it hard, and she had decided to let him down gradually. Still, it meant that he and his father were sharing Sheila's circular Hollywood bed. It left him with a vile taste.

Until Wednesday, September 14th. On that day Dane phoned his mother to ask how she was. She was fine, Lutetia said, although disappointed.

"Your father and I were planning to lunch together downtown," Lutetia said. "While we were discussing it

48

at breakfast, there was phone call from Washington. It was the President's appointments secretary. The President wanted to see Ashton today, so there went our plans." She laughed her tinkly laugh. "I must say Father didn't seem to appreciate the honor. He was actually annoyed. Almost balked at letting me pack his overnight bag. In the end, of course, he went. You don't turn down the President of the United States."

Overnight bag . . .

"Sheila."

"Dane? Hi, darling!"

"See you tonight?"

"Well . . ."

"How about dinner at Louis's?"

"All right, dear, but let's make it early. I'll have to be back before ten."

"How come?"

"I still have gobs of work to do on my designs before the collection is finished."

He could not help wondering what she would use as an excuse after her collection was completed. At the same time, he was puzzled. Overnight bag . . . Had the whole story of the presidential call been a put-up job? Or just the part about presidential overnight?

They had Louis's special salad, which was not on the menu, but Sheila ate it as if it had been prepared by a diner chef. He was asked please not to dawdle over his coffee. They were on the sidewalk at 9:30.

"How about a nightcap, Sheila? A quick one?"

She apparently could not find a plausible way to refuse. Upstairs: "Would you make it yourself, darling? Nothing for me. I'll just change into my working clothes, then you'll have to go."

Calmly Dane said, "I'm not going."

Sheila laughed. "Come on, pardner, have your drink and skedaddle."

"I don't want a drink. And I'm not going."

Her laugh turned uncertain. "Dane, I'm not sure I like this. I must get to work."

"You're not going to work, and I'm not leaving."

"I don't understand. What do you mean?"

"You're trying to get rid of me. I'm not going to be got rid of."

For a moment Sheila was quiet, as if weighing certain factors against her temper. Then she said in a light voice, "Listen to the man! Are you keeping me, O Lord and Master? I pay my own rent, buddy-boy, and you stay when I say, and you leave when I tell you to, and right now I want you to leave." When he stood there, saying nothing, her face turned to ice. "Dane, leave now. I mean *now*. Or you'll be sorry."

"My father will be here any minute, won't he?"

It was if he had struck her. "You know! . . . I suppose you've known all along. I see, I see now. That's why—"

"That's why I'm staying. Yes, sweetie pie, that's why."

He was disgusted with her and with himself and with his father and even with his mother. He stripped off his jacket and laid it across the back of an armchair, and his silver cigaret case, a gift from his mother, dropped out of the pocket. He picked it up and took a cigaret and found his hands shaking so badly he could not light up.

"I'm waiting for my father," he muttered, tossing the case on the chair. "What's more, I intend to tell him about you and me."

With a smothered half-cry, Sheila went to the picture window, to the door, back to the middle of the room. "All right, Dane. Stay and be damned to you. I can't very well put you out by force."

"You didn't have the guts to tell him. Or maybe you never meant to?"

"That's foul, Dane. That really is!"

"One man at a time, I believe you said. Didn't you mean one family at a time?"

To his stupefaction, she burst out laughing. "This is very funny. Funnier than you could possibly imagine!"

"You have a peculiar sense of humor!" Every speck of the love he had felt for her was vanishing with the speed of light. Dread began heavily to build up, and with it the insane rage he had been guarding against.

"You think I've been sleeping with your father?" Sheila cried. "Let me tell you something, little boy—we aren't lovers; we never have been. There's nothing in the least physical about our friendship. Yes, and that's exactly what it is—friendship! We like each other. We respect each other. We enjoy each other's company. But that's all. Of course you won't believe it. Maybe nobody would. But, so help me, Dane, it's the truth. For your own sake, if for no one else's, you'd better believe that."

He could see his own fists, hear his own shout. "Can't you think of a more convincing story that *that*? Friendship! Don't you think I know the old man's been parking his shoes under your bed every Wednesday night? I've seen some of his clothes in your bedroom closet!"

"He's been coming here, yes, and he keeps a change of clothing—some comfortable things—"

"To talk over the little events of the week, I suppose, over a tea cozy? In slacks and a dressing gown? What kind of triple-headed idiot do you take me for? For God's sake, don't you have the decency to admit it when you're caught with your pants down?"

He choked; there was a roaring in his ears. He became faintly aware that her lips were moving.

"I don't want to hurt you, Dane. I don't want to say things about—"

"You'd better not," he heard himself growl.

"—about your mother. But apparently I offer your father a . . . a scope, an experience, that makes it possible for him to talk to me in a way in which he could never talk to his wife. We have a very special and wonderful relationship. It *helps* him to come here every Wednesday night, Dane. And I'm terribly fond of him."

"Why am I bothering? Helps him! How? Come on, spin a few more of your lies to me!"

She flared up at that. "It helps his feelings about himself as a man, if you must know—a man in relation to women. I tell you, Dane, he's my friend, not my lover! He couldn't be my lover even if he wanted to! There! Are you satisfied now? Now do you understand?"

Dane stood dumb. *He couldn't be my lover even if he wanted to . . .*

"You mean you won't let him be? Is that your yarn?"

She said, white-lipped, "I mean he's physically incapable of it. Now you know."

He could not—could not—believe it. Ashton McKell, big, hairy, strapping, vigorous, virile Ashton McKell, incapable of physical relations with a woman?

He sank onto the ottoman, dazed. The very shock of

51

the thought generated its own believability. Nobody, not even a witch, would invent a story like that about Ash McKell. It had to be true. And suddenly he saw how far this went toward explaining the thrusting McKell drive in business, his tapeworm hunger for commercial expansion. A compensation!

But if that were the case, why hadn't his mother said anything? The question answered itself. Lutetia McKell could not have brought herself to mention a thing like that, to her son above all people.

"So now you know the truth," Sheila was saying, and she sounded urgent. "Dane, please, won't you go? I've been trying to find a way to tell your father about you and me without hurting him. Let me work this out my own way. Help me spare him."

He shook his head violently. "I'm going to tell him myself. I've got to know whether this is all true or not."

She clapped her hands in sheer exasperation. "You'd do that? You'd leave him not one shred of self-respect? His own son! Don't you know how ashamed he is of his impotence? Dane, if you do that, you're a rotten, despicable—"

He flung out his arm. "You bitch! Don't call me names!"

"*Bitch*?" Sheila screamed. "Get out of my apartment! Now!"

"No!"

She slapped him with all her might.

And then it came. With a rush.

She was not aware at first what her slap had loosed. For she had started for the house phone. "You leave me no choice. I'm calling John Leslie up here to get you out. I never want to see you again."

From childhood the great flaw in his make-up had been his temper. It had been a hair-trigger thing, exploding at his governess, the servants, other children, his mother—although never his father. Ashton had blamed Lutetia ("You've spoiled him") and hoped that the other boys in boarding school would whip him regularly enough to cure him. But his rages had seemed to feed on violence; and it was not until he was an upperclassman at college that Dane had taught himself restraint. But the lava of his temper was always boiling under his skin.

Now Sheila's hot words, his own guilts, the underlying fear of the confrontation with his father, made him erupt. He leaped at Sheila, whirled her about, and seized her by the throat. He felt, rather than heard, his own voice rumbling, jeering, cursing, choking with hate.

Sheila struggled; her resistance fed his fury. His fingers tightened . . . It was not until her face turned livid, her cries became gurgles, her eyes glassed over and she went suddenly sodden under his hands—it was not until then that a shudder shook him and awareness returned.

Sheila lay collapsed on the floor, barely able to support herself on her forearms, breathing in great gasps. But breathing. Dane stared down at her. There was nothing he could say. It was all over between them. How could she ever look at him again without fear?

His plans—to help his mother—punish his father—marry Sheila . . . all, they were all strangled by that single burst of homicidal fury. What was any of them worth now?

She was alive. He could at least take satisfaction in that.

Dane seized his coat and ran.

Sheila got to her knees, pulled herself erect, toppled onto the ottoman.

She spent some time learning to swallow again, her hands trembling on her bruised throat. She felt cold and sick; her body was racked with shudders. Gradually they subsided, her gasps became normal breathing, her racing heart slowed down.

The thought kept hammering in her head: He almost *killed* me. He wanted to; it was in his murderous eyes . . . Little things came back to her. Hadn't there been signs? His unnatural sulkiness when thwarted? His easy excitability? His inexplicable silences?

Quivering, Sheila scrambled up and went to the bathroom and turned on the cold-water tap. She was drying herself when she heard a key in her door.

It was Ashton McKell.

He looked tired. But his face lit up as he saw her.

"Well, the nation's fate is secure for tonight, anyway," he said. "Old Ash McKell has given the President —good evening, Sheila"—he kissed her, sank onto the ottoman—"the benefit of his advice. Now all he has to do is take it. Sheila? Something wrong?"

She shook her head. Her hand was on her throat.

He jumped up and went to her. "What's happened? Why are you holding your throat?"

"Ash . . . I can't tell you."

"Did you hurt yourself?"

"No. No."

"Did someone hurt you?"

"Ash. Please—"

"Let me see your neck."

"Ash, it's nothing, I tell you."

"I don't understand." He was distressed and bewildered.

"Ash, I don't feel well. Would you understand if . . . ?"

"You'd like me to leave?"

Weeping, she nodded. He hesitated, patted her shoulder, picked up his bag and hat, and left.

Sheila looked out her window at the nighttime city for a few minutes after Ashton McKell's departure. All at once she turned away and hurried into her workroom. She pushed a pile of unfinished fashion sketches aside, took a sheet of notepaper and envelope from a drawer, sat down.

She wrote rapidly:

Sept. 14th

Dane McKell tonight asked if he could come up to my apartment for a nightcap. I told him I had work to do, but he insisted. In the apartment he refused to leave and nothing I could say made him do so. I lost my temper and slapped him. He then tried to strangle me. This is not hysteria on my part—he actually tried to strangle me. He took my throat in his hands and squeezed and seemed to be out of his mind with an

54

insane rage. As he choked me he screamed that he was going to kill me and he called me many obscene names. Then he dropped me to the floor and ran out of the apartment. In another minute I would have been dead of strangulation. I am convinced that he is a dangerous person and I repeat his name, Dane McKell. He definitely tried to kill me.

(signed) Sheila Grey

She did not even bother to reread it. She thrust it into an envelope, moistened the gum, sealed it securely, and on the envelope wrote: *To be opened only in the event I die of unnatural causes.* Now she searched her drawer, found a larger envelope, inserted the first envelope into it, sealed the outer one—heavy and yellow—and on its face wrote: *For the Police.* She hesitated, slipped the envelope into a bottom drawer of her desk, bit her lip, shook her head, took the envelope from the drawer, and dropped it on her desk. I'll find a better place for it in the morning, she told herself.

Sheila sat back now, exhausted to the point of nausea. After a moment she got up and went over to an easy chair in a half-stumble and sank into it. Dizzy, sick to her stomach, shocked to the core, she felt as she imagined people feel when they are dying. If I died right here and now, she thought, I wouldn't care.

Her eyes closed . . .

Later, she could not imagine at first why she was in the easy chair. All of a sudden it came back to her. A glance at her watch told her that less than ten minutes had elapsed.

She visited the bathroom again, dipping a washcloth in cold water, bathing her eyes and neck. My God, what a nightmare, she thought.

Sleep was out of the question, creative work. Yet it was either back to her drawing board or to bed with a sleeping pill, unless . . . Routine, that was it. There were always mindless matters to lose oneself in, rituals of invoice checking, sample matching, note jotting . . .

It was as if she had reached a refuge on her hands and knees. Sheila sat down once more at the desk in her workroom.

This affair had turned out monstrously, monstrously. The best thing to do was to forget it (could she ever forget the clutch of those fingers on her throat?). And she reached for a pile of papers in the desk bin.

Her hand remained in midair.

Someone was in her living room.

Her hand felt paralyzed. She forced it—a sheer act of will—to move toward the telephone, watching it as if it were part of someone else's body. One fingertip clawed at the dial, pulled.

Whoever it was moved stealthily. From the living room into the bedroom.

Far off, a voice spoke. Sheila started. It was in her ear.

Operator." She tried to keep her voice steady in its whisper. *"Police. Quick."*

"Is this an emergency?"

"Yes."

Sheila's teeth chattered on the sibilant. Then there was no sound but the air-conditioner. Then a man's voice said, "Seventeenth Precinct, Sergeant Tumelty."

"Someone is in my apartment."

"Who is this please? What's your address, phone number?"

Sheila told him. "Just hurry," she whispered.

"Don't panic, Miss Grey. Lock the door of the room you're in. We'll have somebody—"

"It's too late!" screamed Sheila. *"No—no—don't shoot—!"*

At the sound of the shot Sergeant Tumelty automatically jotted down the time, 10:23 P.M., and said sharply, "Miss Grey? Was that a shot, or . . . ?"

He recognized the next sound. It was the snick of a receiver being set down on its cradle.

The sergeant got busy.

Just after midnight Dane, seeing the lighted windows in his parents' apartment, went up and found his mother alone in the music room, watching an old film on television, *Quality Street*, from James Barrie's 1901 drama of manners. No buckets of blood for Lutetia. In spite of Dane's protest she turned off the set.

She kissed him on the brow. "Wouldn't you like something to eat, dear? Or some cold lemonade?"

"No, thanks, Mother. Father's not back?"

"No. I suppose he got through too late in Washington. After all, he did take an overnight bag."

"And what have you been doing with yourself?" Dane wandered idly about the music room.

"Being just too wickedly slothful. The servants left at eight, and I've been sitting here ever since watching the television."

"Mother?"

"Yes, dear," smiled Lutetia.

"I've got something to ask you. Something very personal."

"Oh?" She looked puzzled. The specific area of his question would never occur to her even as a speculation.

"I hope you understand that I wouldn't ask such a thing if it weren't very important for me to know." He was casting about for some "nice" way to phrase the question.

"Of course, dear." She laughed uncertainly. "You do make it sound . . . well . . ."

The way occurred to him. "Do you recall the annulment of the Van Der Broekyns marriage?" She immediately turned pink; she remembered. "His second marriage?" Lutetia nodded reluctantly. "What I have to ask you is this: Has it been, well, that same way with Dad?"

"Dane! How dare you!"

"I'm sorry, Mother. I must know. Has it?"

She refused to meet his eyes; sitting there, she was actually wringing her hands.

"Has it?"

He could barely hear her "Yes."

And he was astounded. It was true. Sheila had told

him the literal truth. He had never been so bewildered in his life.

"But Mother, I don't understand. Why didn't you tell me this before, when we were discussing . . . ?"

"There are some things one simply doesn't reveal," Lutetia said stiffly, "even to one's children. Especially to one's children."

"Mother, I'm not a child any more. I've known the facts of life for a long time, although my upbringing in that respect has been more like that of a tulip." His bitterness was beginning to well up. He bit his lips, and the pain calmed down. "If Dad's had this, well, condition, you tell me how he could have been unfaithful to you, as you said."

"Infidelity is not just . . . physical." Her lips were drawn up in a snarl of tension. "There's infidelity of the spirit as well. Your father's father and mother lived together for fifty-one years without having to find another woman or man."

"Mother, Mother."

He studied her, at a loss. How could he have arrived at his age knowing so little about his parents? His father, with problems both physical and psychological Dane could now only begin to guess at, going through his elaborate monkeyshines—drawn car shades, changed clothes, disguise, like some character out of E. Phillips Oppenheim or Conan Doyle—merely to visit another woman he could not even sleep with; his mother, tormented with such cloudy concepts as "infidelity of the spirit" to cover her outraged Victorian feelings . . .

"Mother." He went over to her, stooped, took her hands. "I'm just beginning to realize how awful this must be for you. Would you like me to stay overnight?"

She busied herself preparing his old room with the zest of a woman welcoming back one of her menfolk after a three-year whaling cruise. They kissed and parted for the night. He lay in bed staring at the college banners on the wall. His mother, he knew, was on her knees in her room, praying; he envied her. His thoughts ranged afield, but kept coming back to Sheila Grey. What was he feeling so persistently and profoundly? Uncleanliness? Indecency? Revulsion?

For his actions of the evening, search as he might, he could find no trace of justification.

The next morning, dressing, thinking it would soon be fall and that he had hoped to have his book finished by the end of the year—a goal that now seemed parsecs away—Dane hunted for a cigaret. The box on the bed table was empty, and he went through his coat pockets.

He found a crumpled pack of cigarets, but no cigaret case. His silver cigaret case was missing. With a thump of his heart he realized that he could not recall having seen it or felt it after visiting Sheila's the night before.

He found his lighter and lit one of the out-of-shape cigarets—one sock on, the other off—telling himself: Forget her. *Forget her.*

After a while, hands shaking badly, he finished dressing.

He almost cried out when he walked into the dining room. His father was seated at the table drinking coffee. When had he come in? And with what story? The elder McKell looked haggard, as if he had not slept; his clothes were wrinkled. This was unprecedented.

"Morning, Dad. How was your trip?"

"All right." Ashton's voice seemed stifled. His eyes, Dane noted now, were bloodshot. He raised his coffee cup, set it down, moved the saucer, fiddled with the sugar tongs. Dane was relieved when his mother joined them.

She was paler than usual this morning. It was evident that she had already talked to her husband. Dane wondered what he had told her, what she had said to him.

But beyond brief, almost formal, exchanges, breakfast was consumed in silence. Looking up from his eggs from time to time, Dane would catch his father's eye; the eye would immediately move elsewhere. Dane tried to interpret the look. Baleful? Reproachful? Secretive? Frightened? He grew uneasy. It's time the curtain came down on this whole thing, Dane thought, feeling his temper rise, pushing it back down, sitting on it. Not that again.

"Well!" Ashton McKell said abruptly. "This table is about as lively as Wall Street on Sunday morning." His whole demeanor had changed. "And it's my fault. I've been working too hard. I'm worn out. Lutetia, what would you say to a trip somewhere? Just the two of us? A pleasure trip?"

"Ashton!"

"Now that the tourists are coming home, we could go to Europe. No business—just sightseeing with the rest of the rubbernecks from the States. I promise I wouldn't visit a single branch office or customer."

"Oh, Ashton, that would be simply lovely. When would you plan to go?"

"Why not now?" The tycoon's lips were taut. "We can leave as soon as we get a good boat. One of the *Queens*. I'll arrange for passage this morning. No flying this time—a leisurely sea crossing—"

"Let's go to Paris first!" cried Lutetia. "Where shall we stay?"

They chattered away about plans like newlyweds. So Sheila had been telling the truth about that, too. She had been tapering him off, letting him down gently, and at last he had got the message. Or was it something else—?

"We've never been to Luxembourg," Ashton said enthusiastically. "—Yes, Ramon?"

"The car is ready, Mr. McKell," the chauffeur said.

"Wait for me."

"What is it, Margaret?" asked Lutetia. Ramon withdrew, and old Margaret, the senior maid, had come in.

"Callers, ma'am."

"At this hour? Who are they?"

"Policemen, ma'am."

"Policemen?"

The roaring began in Dane's ears. He barely heard his father say, "Show them in, Margaret. Lu, you let me handle this—you, too, Dane"; was barely conscious of the entrance of two men in plainclothes, one of them a giant of a man with a gravelly voice.

"I'm Sergeant Velie of police headquarters," the big man said, flipping open his shield case. "This is Detective Mack of the 17th Precinct. I'm sorry to disturb you so early in the morning, but you know what's happened in this building—"

60

"Happened?" Ashton McKell was on his feet. "No, Sergeant, we didn't know. What is it?"

"The tenant of the penthouse, Miss Grey, was murdered a little before half-past ten last night."

Lutetia McKell was slewed around, one delicate hand gripping the back of her chair; her husband's pallor took on a corpselike lividity. Dane fought down the ugly and familiar roaring by sheer savagery.

"What we want to know, sir," Sergeant Velie was saying, "is if you people heard anything around the time of the murder . . ."

Ashton McKell's knees buckled and he pitched over with a thud.

II. The Second Side

ASHTON

The two policemen picked up Ashton McKell and carried him to the couch, loosened his clothing. Dane did nothing.

"You maybe ought to call a doctor, Mrs. McKell," the bigger detective said.

She shook her head. From somewhere she had produced a silver filigree smelling-salts bottle and she was holding it to her husband's ashy nose. He twitched, trying to get away from it. She pursued him with firmness. "It's just overwork. My husband works too hard, and then this shock on top of it . . . Only yesterday he was called to Washington by the President. Last week he had to fly down to South America. We were just talking about a vacation . . . Murdered, you say? That poor woman. No, we didn't hear anything; this is an old house with very thick walls and floors. Dane, please fetch a glass of water from the kitchen. Don't say anything to the servants. There's no point in distressing them."

She continued to talk. It seemed the most natural thing in the world, listening to her, that her husband should have fainted on hearing of a tenant's violent death.

Gradually his color returned; his eyelids fluttered. Lutetia rose and faced the detectives.

"You've been very kind. It's all right now. I know we mustn't keep you gentlemen."

"We'll probably have to come back," the big sergeant said with an air of apology. The officers left.

Dane had brought the water in a daze. He sat down at the table, trying to master his nerves, which seemed to have been invaded by St. Vitus. All the little muscles in his hands and face were twittering. He knew he would never forget the sight of his father's face, this morning of September 15th, drawn even before the detectives' visit, turning clay-colored as the announcement came and his eyes turned over and he slid to the floor. Had his father ever before in his life fainted? Dane was sure he had not. The news of Sheila Grey's death must have been a tremendous shock.

The two detectives . . . the tall one with the sledge-hammer hands and the rumbling voice who did all the talking—what was his name again? Sergeant Velie—were deference and concern his usual attitudes on the job? Dane thought not. All detectives had to be actors or a sort, and it seemed to Dane that Sergeant Velie had been striding the boards in full make-up. He knew something. Far more than he had let on.

Dane reached for a cigaret. Then it came back to him: he had not been able to find his cigaret case earlier this morning, just the remains of an old pack. The flat taste of the cigaret he had smoked seemed still in his mouth. Or was it the taste of fear?

His father had begun to moan; his mother had phoned Dr. Peabody after all and was back at her husband's side; Dane ignored them and ran back to his room. He tumbled things about, questioned the servants, went through the other rooms.

"My cigaret case!" He flung the phrase at his parents. Lutetia looked up; her blue eyes were moist, she was holding on to her husband's hand. "Have you seen my cigaret case?" She shook her head, obviously bewildered that such a thing could be on his mind; as for Ashton McKell, he was now breathing regularly—otherwise, he lay in silence.

Dane collapsed in a chair. His mother—raised in the world of her grandmother, when pipes were Rough, cigars Ostentatious, and cigarets Fast (snuff was regrettably outmoded, while chewing tobacco was not mentioned in polite society)—had given him the silver case on his twenty-first birthday as a sign of grace, conferring the solid right in his new manhood to smoke in her presence without the hint of reproof that had greeted his two or three earlier attempts. The case was a beautifully handcrafted Tiffany piece; the inside of the lid was engraved *Philip Dane DeWitt McKell.*

Where was it?

If he had left it in Sheila's apartment, then the police had found it. The presence of his cigaret case on the scene of the crime . . . He might be able to get by with saying that he had left it there on a previous visit . . . Worry nibbled at him.

If the police had found the case, why hadn't the two

64

detectives mentioned it? Of course, they might be laying a trap for him. On the other hand, suppose they hadn't found it?—because it wasn't there? In that case, what had happened to it?

The next two days were unpleasant. His parents made no further mention of a European tour. Ashton Mc-Kell's manner at home was listless and preoccupied.

Dane tried to work on his book without any success whatever. It was easier to sit turning the pages of illustrated books of other people, the illustrations distracting without requiring concentration—bulky books, Audubon's sketchbooks, volumes of Peter Breughel and Hieronymus Bosch. The Bosch he flung aside; that nightmare world ruined his sleep. Demons, naked women and men, apples . . . silver cigaret cases . . .

There was something besides the cigaret case. For weeks he had been monopolizing Sheila Grey's life—lunches, dinners, the theater, the ballet, walks, ferry rides. *Cherchez l'homme*.

He supposed it worked that way, too. Look for the man. He was the last man in Sheila's life. How long would it take the police, by routine legwork, to get around to him?

He found it childishly easy to yield to his mother's plea that for the present he take his meals with her and his father. He wondered if she knew, or suspected, about him and Sheila.

They were at breakfast, a moody one, his father's *New York Times* untouched beside his plate, when the two police officers returned. One look at their faces told Dane that it was no longer a matter of questions like *Did you hear anything unusual*, etc.

Again it was Sergeant Velie who did all the talking. He greeted Lutetia politely, nodded to Dane. But his attention was concentrated on Ashton McKell.

They had all risen; the sergeant waved them back, refused a chair, and said, "On this Sheila Grey murder. I can tell you she was shot through the heart"—a stifled sound from Lutetia, and Ashton gripped her hand with-

out taking his eyes off the officer—"and was killed instantly. A .38 S. & W. Terrier revolver was found next
to the body. You want to say something, Mr. McKell?"

Ashton said quickly, "That's probably my gun, Sergeant. There's no mystery about it if it is, although of
course you want an explanation. I lent it to Miss Grey.
She said she was sometimes nervous being all alone in
the penthouse. At the same time I didn't want a frightened woman handling a loaded gun. So I filled the
chambers with blanks without mentioning it to her—it
was more to give her confidence than anything else. Do
you mean to say . . . ?"

"Say what, Mr. McKell?"

"That Miss Grey was shot with my gun?"

"Yes."

"But it was loaded with blanks! I loaded it myself!"

"It was no blank," Sergeant Velie said, "that killed
her."

"I don't know how it could have been replaced,"
Ashton McKell said in a calm voice—was there the
slightest tremor?—"or by whom. For all I know Miss
Grey may have done it herself. I don't know how much
she knew about firearms."

Sergeant Velie was looking at him with great steadi-
ness. "Let's skip the gun and bullets for now. You admit
you knew the woman?"

"There's nothing to admit. Of course I knew Miss
Grey. I know all the tenants in this building. I own it."

"You knew her well?"

"Who?"

"Miss Grey," the sergeant said patiently.

"Quite well."

"And how well would quite well be, Mr. McKell?"
Dane glanced at his mother. She was absolutely rigid.

"I don't know what you mean, Sergeant."

Velie said, "You see, sir, we found men's clothing in
her apartment. One man's clothing." The sergeant
paused, then repeated, "You want to say something, Mr.
McKell?"

The elder McKell nodded with remarkable self-pos-
session. He did not look at his wife. "They're my
clothes, Sergeant," he said quietly. "You must have
traced them."

66

"That's right, we did. We checked out the tailor's labels and the laundry marks, and so forth. Anything else you have to say to us?"

Lutetia's face was now expressionless. Their hands were still tightly gripped, Dane noticed.

At this moment Ramon came in. "Sir, excuse me," he said to Ashton McKell, "but the Bentley will not start. Shall I use the Continental, or . . . ?"

"Never mind, Ramon. Wait in the kitchen, please. Mrs. McKell may need you."

Ramon withdrew in impervious silence. In Spain, where he had been born and trained, servants did not ask questions.

Dane was thinking: His clothing . . . What kind of relationship *had* they had? It sounded like something out of Havelock Ellis. And how could it have satisfied Sheila? The raging wave stirred. He went to work on it . . .

"You're leading up to something, Sergeant Velie," his father was saying steadily. "I'd appreciate your coming to the point." Dane felt weak and ill.

Sergeant Velie continued to regard Ashton McKell with that same impaling glance. Dane knew what the sergeant was thinking, what had brought him and the other detective to the McKell apartment this morning. Ashton McKell had had the means to commit the murder: it was his revolver that had taken Sheila Grey's life; his story about the blanks was not substantiated by the facts, and in any case it sounded feeble. He had had opportunity: he and Sheila Grey occupied the same building. He had had motive (but here Dane's brain shut down; he refused to think of theoretical motive, kept pushing it back and away, out of sight).

Lutetia's delicate face was cameo-white, cameo-stone.

"Mr. McKell, I'm going to have to ask you to come downtown for further questioning. You won't need your car. We've got a police car at the side entrance." So much was granted Ashton McKell's position in society. The tumbril awaits . . . but at the tradesmen's entrance.

Ashton's face was stone, too. "All right, Sergeant," he said. He disengaged his hand gently. "Lutetia, I'm sorry," he said in a very low voice. She did not reply, but her eyes flew open wide, very wide. "Son—"

Dane moistened his dried-out lips. "Don't worry, Dad. We'll get you out of this right away."

"Take care of your mother, son. By the way, I forgot a handkerchief this morning. May I have yours?"

On this absurd note Ashton McKell left between the two policemen. After the apartment door snicked shut with guillotine finality, Dane turned back to his mother. She was no longer there. He went to her bedroom and called out, but there was no response. He tried her door; it was locked. After a moment he went to the phone.

Ashton McKell had a staff of six attorneys at his New York headquarters. Dane called none of them. Richard M. Heaton was the McKell family lawyer.

"Almighty God!" said Richard M. Heaten.

Hanging up, Dane felt himself sweating in the air-conditioned apartment. He felt for his handkerchief and remembered that he had given it to his father. Abstractedly he went to his room and opened the handkerchief drawer of his old bureau.

His hand remained in midair.

His silver cigaret case lay on one of the piles of handkerchiefs.

The silver case had been removed from the penthouse before the police got there. Who could have removed it? Obviously, the same one who had placed it here, in his bureau drawer . . . his father. That was why Ashton McKell had "forgotten" his own handkerchief (as if he ever forgot an essential article of clothing!) and borrowed Dane's: to make Dane go to his room for a replacement and, as a consequence, to find the cigaret case. His father must have seen it in Sheila's apartment, recognized it, pocketed it, and only now placed it in Dane's bureau.

What a bitter night it must have been for him, Dane thought. Finding the evidence of Dane's presence on Sheila's premises, he must have realized in a flash why

68

Sheila was easing him out of her life. His own son . . .

And the king went to the tower which was by the gate, and as he went, thus he said, My son, my son, Absalom. My son, my son, Absalom. Would God I died for thee, O Absalom, my son, my son.

Absalom had conspired against David, his father. Suddenly Dane saw Ashton McKell in a very different light from the clownish spectacle of the man who skulked in out-of-the-way places disguising himself in order to visit a woman he could not even embrace. In his blackest hour—an almost-criminal on the brink of scandal, his life in danger—his parting thought had been for the son who had betrayed him, his last directive an unspoken *Don't worry, son, I've retrieved your case from the penthouse, now they can't place you on the scene.*

And Dane sat down in his childhood rocker and wept.

In a city in which murder is hamburgers by the dozen, the McKell arrest was caviar to the general. Not often did a case break in which the accused was tycoon, adviser to presidents, prince of commerce, son of a name who was son of a name untainted for generations, and all rolled into one man.

If Lutetia McKell's anguish at the wild invasion of her privacy by the press was not quite on a level with her horror at Ashton's predicament, it was still powerful enough to dominate her household. She had caught a single glimpse of a single tabloid (left incautiously in the kitchen by old Margaret, whose open vice was the journalism of murder and rape); it was enough. All newspapers, even the *New York Times,* were banned from the premises; and when it became evident that the scavengers of the press, in particular the photographers, were laying siege to the building, Lutetia went into strictest seclusion, like a Hindu widow, and forbade the entrance of the clamoring world by so much as an uncurtained window. To reach his mother, Dane found himself having to follow a route he had not used since his boyhood, entering another building around the corner, descending to its basement, and emerging into the alley from which he could reach the apartment of John Leslie, the doorman, by a window. John or his wife would let him in, and then out by the basement door adjacent to the service elevator. It had been great fun when he was a youngster, but somehow the adventure had lost its savor. When it became necessary to confer with Lawyer Heaton, Lutetia reacted to Heaton's suggestion that she and Dane visit his office as if he had invited her to take a sunbath naked on the roof.

"I shall not set foot outside this apartment," she said, in tears. "Nothing, nothing can make me!"

So stately Mahomet came to the mountain; and indeed it was almost as traumatic an experience for Richard M. Heaton as it would have been for Lutetia. For Heaton was the very portrait of the trusted family lawyer—elderly, florid, with the dignity of a retired major-general, and as horror-struck by the notion of publicity as Lutetia herself. He gained entry to the McKell building in a slightly disheveled condition after running the gauntlet of newsmen, and from his distress he might have been stripped by their waving hands to his underclothing.

"Foul beasts," he muttered, accepting a glass of sherry and a biscuit from Lutetia in great agitation. He wore a resentful look, as if he had been tricked. It took Dane five minutes to calm him.

"This is quite beyond my depth, Lutetia," he said at last. "I have had no occasion to practice criminal law—haven't appeared in court for any reason in fifteen years. What a dreadful business! A dressmaker!" Dane was tempted to ask him if he would have felt better about the whole mess if Sheila Grey's name had been Van Spuyten, the end result of a long line of patroons. But he did not, for he suspected that his mother felt very much the same way.

"Tell Mother what you told me, Mr. Heaton."

"Why I haven't been able to pry your father out of the hands of the police? Well, Lutetia, Ashton cannot prove an alibi. He has told the authorities where he was at the time of the—of the event, but they're unable to corroborate it. Therefore, they are continuing to hold him. Now. Although the charge is the most serious one under the law—with the possible exception of treason, of course, and the last treason indictment I can remember anywhere is that against John Brown by the State of Virginia—"

"Mr. Heaton," said Dane politely, but firmly. He could see that his mother was holding herself together by sheer heroism.

"I'm rambling, forgive me, Lutetia. This has upset me more than I can say. However, even though murder is among the gravest of charges, an accused is presumed innocent until proved guilty, thank God, and I do not for one moment suppose such proof can be obtained in this case."

"Then why haven't you been able to get Ashton's release on bond?" Lutetia asked timidly. "Dane tells me you said that New York State allows bond even in a charge of first—in a first-degree charge."

"It's complicated," sighed Richard M. Heaton. "We have fallen afoul of a very poor climate, politically speaking, on the bail question, I mean here in the city. Of course, you don't follow such things, but only a few months ago there was the case of another, ah, of a very prominent man who shot his wife to death. He was released on $100,000 bail, and he promptly fled the country. It has made the courts and the district attorney's office extremely shy where bond in capital cases is concerned, especially since the newspapers have raked up the other case and are asking quite maliciously if this will prove a repetition."

"But Ashton wouldn't do a thing like that," Lutetia moaned. "Richard, he's *innocent*. Only guilty men flee. It isn't *fair*."

"I'm afraid we don't live in as ideal a democracy as we sometimes boast," the old lawyer said sadly. "The rich and socially prominent are very often discriminated against in our society. We could probably force the issue in the courts, but the trouble is . . ." He hesitated.

"The trouble is what, Mr. Heaton?" Dane asked sharply.

"Your father seems reluctant to battle it out legally. In fact, he's all but forbidden me to."

"What!"

"But why?" asked Lutetia blankly.

"Why indeed? In view of the state of public opinion, he seems to feel that it would be wiser not to press for bail. He actually told me, 'Perhaps the public is right. If I were a poor man I wouldn't be able to raise the kind of bail that would be set in a case like this. Let it go.' I must confess I hadn't expected such a thoroughly unrealistic attitude from Ashton McKell, and I told him so. A martyr's attitude will avail him nothing, nothing at all."

Lutetia sniffed into her tiny bit of cambric. "Ashton has always been so principled. But I do wish . . ." Then she cried quietly.

Dane comforted her, thinking that neither she nor the lawyer had caught the point. Perhaps Ashton himself was not aware of it. Though his father continued to insist quite rationally on his innocence of the murder charge, he was carrying a heavy load of guilt around for another crime; and of this one he was guilty as hell—consorting, as Lutetia would have termed it, with another woman. It was not as if he despised his wife and, in despising her, sought a more loving pair of arms, bought or offered gratis. Ashton did not despite Lutetia; he loved her. It was like loving a piece of fragile chinaware, the slightest jar to which would crack it. He had been responsible for cracking the delicate image, and he must be feeling the same sort of shame and guilt as if, in fact, he had been contemptuous of it.

Dane went to see his father. The elder McKell looked like a hollow reproduction of himself—as if he had had his stuffing scooped out. Dane could hardly bear to look at him.

Ashton asked, in tones softer than Dane could remember, "Son, how are you? How is your mother?"

"We're fine. The question is, Dad, how are you?"

"This is all a dream, and I'll soon wake up. But then I know I'm awake—that the past was the dream. It's something like that, son."

They chatted awkwardly for a while, about Lutetia chiefly, how she was reacting to her overturned world. Finally Dane got around to the object of his visit. "Dad, I want you to tell me all about that night—what you did, where you went. In detail. Just as you told the police."

"If you want me to, Dane." The elder man considered for a moment, sighing. "I got to the penthouse just before ten o'clock—the cab was held up by an accident on the highway, or it would have been sooner. The traffic from the airport isn't very heady at that hour."

About ten o'clock. It would have been mere minutes after he himself had left her alive in the penthouse.

"I didn't stay long. She was terribly upset. By what she wouldn't say."

Dane bent over the pad, on which he was taking notes, to cover his wince. "How long were you there, Dad? As exactly as you can recall."

"She asked me to leave almost at once, so I did. I couldn't have been there more than several minutes. I'd say I left at 10:03 at the latest."

"Where did you go from there?"

Ashton said quietly, "I was rather upset myself. I walked."

"Where? For how long?" And why didn't I ask him why he was upset? Dane thought. Because I know, that's why . . .

"I just don't remember. It couldn't have been too long, I suppose. I do remember being in a bar—"

"What bar?"

"I don't know. I had a drink and talked to the bartender, I remember that."

"You're sure you don't know where the bar is?"

"Not even approximately, although for some reason First Avenue sticks in my head. But I can't honestly say it was there. Somewhere in the Sixties—I think. A side street, I seem to recall that, anyway. I was simply not paying any attention to things like that." A ghost of a smile touched the rocky face. "I certainly wish now that I had."

"And you didn't notice the name of the bar?"

"Or I've forgotten. You know, a lot of those little place have no names. Just *Bar*."

"Have you an idea how long you were in there?"

"Quite a while. More than a few minutes. I do remember leaving the place and walking some more. Finally I took a cab—"

"I don't suppose you remember the cabbie's name or number."

"God, no. Or when, or where, or what street I got out at. I remember getting out some blocks short of home because I suddenly wanted air. I walked the rest of the way."

"And you can't even recall what time it was when you got home?"

"I haven't the foggiest idea, Dane." Dane knew that his mother did not know, either, for she had told him, "I didn't know your father was home until early morning, when I woke up."

"I'm afraid, son, the information isn't of any use."

Dane wanted to talk about his father's having replaced the silver cigaret case; he had even thought of bringing up the whole business of his relationship with Sheila Grey; but just then the turnkey terminated his visit. The street was steaming with gasoline fumes and oily vapors, but the air seemed sweetly pure after the jail.

He went over to police headquarters and got in to see the man in charge of several phases of the Grey investigation, a birdy little man with a gray brush mustache, an inspector named Queen.

"Take a load off your feet, Mr. McKell," said Inspector Queen, nodding toward a chair of rivuleted black leather, "and listen to the gospel. We have to go by the weight of the circumstantial evidence. The weight of the circumstantial evidence is against your father. Ballistics says the bullet that killed her came from the gun your father admits belongs to him—not that it's important whether he admits it or not; his ownership is a matter of record. He was admittedly on the scene within minutes of the exact moment of the shooting as recorded by the desk sergeant of the 17th Precinct, from hearing the shot over the phone. And while the State doesn't have to prove motive, it comes in handy, and your father's motive sticks in the old slot they all stick in when a man is having an affair with a woman not his wife—sorry I have to be blunt, but there it is. And all he offers us in rebuttal is this yarn about having been in a bar. But what bar, where, when, he can't tell us."

Dane wondered what this little briar of an inspector would say if he were to be told about the disguise and the impotence. Probably, he thought, boot me out of here for telling bad jokes so early in the day.

"Have you tried to check out his story, Inspector?"

The Inspector said explosively, "People give me a pain. I forgive you because it's your father who's involved, and people don't think straight when they're upset. My dear Mr. McKell, you don't suppose we collect bonuses for every indictment the grand jury brings in, do you? Like fox tails in chicken country? Of course we checked it out. Or tried our damnedest to. You know how many bars there are in every square mile of Manhattan Island? I've got a pile of reports here that make my feet ache just looking at 'em.

"We checked every last bar in the neighborhood your father mentioned, and not just in the Sixties, or on First Avenue, either. We hit that whole midtown East Side area in a saturation investigation. Nobody—but *nobody* —remembers having seen him that night; and our men carried photographs. That night or any other night, I might add. So what do you suggest we do? I'm sorry, Mr. McKell, but my advice to you is to get your father the best trial lawyers money can hire."

Dane McKell did not know what the police could or could not do, but he knew what he had to do. He had to find that bar. He went back to his parents' home, fished in the family album and, armed with a photograph of his father, set out in his MG.

He drove from street to street. He was operating on the theory that the police had interpreted "bar" too narrowly; besides, perhaps his father was in confusion or error as to the exact location of the place. The police having covered bars on the East Side midtown, he would widely extend the hunt.

He visited bars, grills, restaurants, oyster houses, steak joints, even hotels; the dark and the light, the new and old and ageless places. "Have you ever seen this man? Are you sure? He might have had a drink in here on the night of September 14th, between ten P.M. and midnight."

In one dim bistro the inevitable happened.

"Sure," the barkeep said. Dane perked up. "He's here right now. Jerry? Here's a guy looking for you." Jerry did bear a resemblance to Ashton McKell, if Ashton McKell had spent his days boozing in a fourth-rate grogshop and shaved every third day.

Dane stumbled over another trail in a place on Second Avenue, in the upper 60s. The barman took one look at Ashton McKell's photo and grunted, "Who is this guy, everybody's rich uncle?"

Dane was tired. "What do you mean?"

"The girl."

"What girl?"

"Ain't she working with you? First she comes in, then you. Nice-looking broad. She was in here a few minutes ago. Nah, I never seen this old duck, and that's what I told her, too."

So a girl was combing the bars with a picture of his father, too! Could she be a policewoman? Dane did not think so. It seemed scarcely the sort of work to which a policewoman would be assigned; besides, that phase of the police investigation had been covered. Then who was she? Could there have been *two* other women in his father's life? By now Dane did not care if there had been a haremful. His own meddling had helped bring his father to a human kennel, his life in jeopardy. Only get him out of there! Nothing else mattered any longer.

The mystery of the girl was solved prosaically enough. Dane had come out of a pink-and-white barroom occupied by slender men in form-fitting clothing and had entered a white-and-pink barroom occupied by women who used too much eye make-up and who looked up quickly as he came in. The bartender was at the other end of the bar, half blocked out by the figure of a woman who was showing him something.

"No, miss," the man was saying. "Not on September 14th or any other night."

Dane moved toward her; she turned around and they almost collided.

"Judy!"

It was Judith Walsh, his father's secretary. He had

seen nothing of Judy since the fateful night; he had supposed that in his father's trouble she was holding down the fort at the McKell offices.

"Dane, what are you doing here?"

"The same thing you are, apparently. Trying to prove Dad's alibi."

He took her to a booth and ordered beers.

"How long have you been at this?" he asked her.

"Seems like ten years," she said disconsolately. "I simply didn't know what else to do. I couldn't just do nothing."

Dane nodded; he knew something—not much—of the story behind her devotion to his father. The elder McKell had given Judith Walsh her first and only job, at a time when she could see for herself nothing but the fate of most girls from her economic class—a hasty and overfertile marriage, and a life of drudgery. She had made herself indispensable to Ashton, and he had repaid her handsomely.

"Look, Judy, we're both pulling on the same oar," Dane said. "Why don't we hook up? What places have you covered?"

"I have a list."

"So have I. Between the two of us, we ought to turn it up."

Judy set down her half-finished beer. "We're wasting time, Dane. Let's get back on it."

They kept going by day and by night; after a while, in a sort of sleepwalking daze. The photographs became cracked and dog-eared.

It was bitterly interesting to see how the news of the indictment handed down by the grand jury affected people Dane knew. A girl who had been in pursuit of him since the spring, phoning him several times a week, vanished from the face of the earth. Friends these days were always hurrying somewhere, unable to chat for more than a minute or two. On the other hand, old Colonel Adolphus Phillipse, Lutetia's cousin, appeared at the McKell apartment for the first time since the funeral of Lutetia's grandmother's sister—pausing en route just long enough to whale away at a cameraman with his walking stick—and announced that he had pawned his mother's jewelry, offering the proceeds, $10,000, as a reward leading to the arrest and conviction of what he termed "the real culprit." He was persuaded with difficulty that his generosity was not needed.

By November 1st, Dane and Judy were worn out, stumped. The only thing they did not doubt was the truth of Ashton McKell's story. As Dane said, "If for no other reason than that, if he'd made the story up, he could hardly have helped inventing a better one!"

And on November 1st, in a crowded courtroom, Judge Edgar Suarez presiding, the trial of Ashton McKell began. It was a Tuesday.

On Wednesday, after another night's fruitless search, not concluded until the bars closed, Dane insisted on taking Judy home to her West End Avenue apartment. Her eyes were deeply stamped with fatigue. Outside her building he said, "You swallow a sleeping pill, missie, and hit the sack."

"No," Judy said. "I want to check off the places we covered tonight against the list of licenses I have upstairs. To make sure we didn't skip one."

She swayed, and he caught her. "Here! I'd better come up and help you tick them off. Then you're going to bed."

He had never been in her apartment before. It was tailored but feminine, with some creditable pieces of bric-à-brac, and an impressive hi-fi set backed up by a formidable collection of recordings.

"All my money goes into it," Judy laughed, noticing his respectful eyebrows. "I'm a frustrated musician, I guess. How are you on music?"

"Long-haired," said Dane.

"Wonderful! Maybe we can spend an evening listening to a whole nightful of music. I mean when this is, well, over."

"I'd like that."

"I have some simply marvelous old 78s. Do you know the prewar Beethoven symphonies recorded by Felix Weingartner and the Vienna Philharmonic? In my opinion they're still the definitive performances . . ."

They checked their list of the evening. In the area they had covered, not one place that sold liquor over a bar had been passed by. "There," Judy said, putting down her pencil. "That's done. Funny, I don't feel as tired—"

Dane took her in his arms, kissed her mouth. After one gasp of surprise, she returned the pressure.

Later, he told himself it had been inevitable. The attraction between them—how old was it? It seemed to him now that it dated from their first sight of each other, years before. He had always been drawn to a certain quality of sweet cleanliness about her, dainty and uncomplicated and altogether feminine. Why hadn't he realized it sooner? And where now was his passion for Sheila Grey? Already her memory was a vestigial relic of the past. Was he so shallow, or had his love for Sheila been no love at all?

But just as suddenly as he had begun making love to Judy, he stopped, pushed her aside, and hurried from her apartment. She was more puzzled than hurt, more tired than puzzled. As she sank into sleep the thought drifted through her head: He feels guilty about being happy while his father is in a mess, that's why. Dane was such a strange man . . .

They established a routine. During the day they attended the trial; the evening and night were dedicated to the hunt for the elusive bar and the invisible bartender. They took their hasty meals together. Judy was aware of a restraint on Dane's part—a hint of wariness, a drawing away. And yet there were times when he seemed to recapture something of those few minutes in her apartment that night. But these were mere glimpses into what had already become a misty remembrance of things past. It was almost as if she had dreamed the whole episode.

A chill invaded the city. The tang of hot chestnut smoke hung about Manhattan street corners, the city's equivalent of suburbia's burning leaves. Through streets fashionable and down-at-heel, clean and dirty, through areas of high-rent apartments and melting-pot neighborhoods and garbage-littered slums, they pressed their search. And still the search went unrewarded.

The trial approached its climax. Few defendants

against a charge of murder had had so distinguished a group of character witnesses as paraded to the stand to testify to the probity and non-lethal nature of Ashton McKell. But Dane knew, and Judith Walsh knew, and Richard M. Heaton knew, and most of all Robert O'Brien knew—the highly capable criminal lawyer associated with Heaton for the defense—for how little all this counted. The district attorney had only to paraphrase the prosecution's words in the Richard Savage case of long ago ("Gentlemen of the jury, you are to consider that Mr. Savage is a much greater man than you or I; that he wears much finer clothes than you or I; and that he has much more money in his pocket than you or I, gentlemen of the jury; but is it not a very hard case, gentlemen of the jury, that he should therefore kill you or me, gentlemen of the jury?") for everyone to see how very little all the fine words by all the fine people added up to.

"What are my father's chances?" Dane asked O'Brien. And O'Brien looked him in the eye and said, "Very poor indeed." Had his answer been anything else, Dane would not have believed him.

Judy wept. "There has to be something else we can do," she wailed, "before it's too late. Couldn't you hire a private detective, Dane?"

"To do what?" His laugh was more of a bark. "Show them anything out of the ordinary and they're afraid to touch it. Oh, it wouldn't be hard to find one who'd take the money, but . . ." And just then something slipped to the surface of his mind.

It was the name of a man he had met once at a literary cocktail party in the Algonquin. A man who wrote detective stories for a living, and for a hobby . . . there were some impressive, if incredible, stories in circulation about his hobby. And wasn't his father connected with the New York police?

"By God!" Dane exclaimed. "His father is that old man I talked to at police headquarters!"

"Whose father?" Judy asked, puzzled.

"I know just the fellow!"

So they went to look for Ellery Queen.

They found Ellery in the private pavilion of the Swedish-Norwegian Hospital in Murray Hill.

"We squareheads are very adept at patching up ski accident cases," genial Dr. Johanneson had said, patting the casts in which Ellery was immobilized.

"You ought to be," Ellery growled, "you invented the damned things. And don't look so pleased with yourself. I'll have you know the Queens were breaking their bones in civilized ways when your barbarian ancestors were still chiseling runes in the forests of Gothland!"

It was a pleasant enough room, the walls painted a tonic yellow-sand. Ellery regarded his two young visitors quizzically. "This just isn't my year," he complained. "I'd gone up to Wrightsville to get in some early skiing. It was my luck that a movie outfit was shooting winter scenes in the Mahoganies and the director, a man I know, wheedled me into the act. The crew had rigged a camera on a bobsled, the bobsled broke loose, and next thing I knew, as I came downslope the sled and I had an argument. You know, I don't so much mind the leg that was broken by the sled. It's the one my own skis broke that bugs me! How's your latest novel coming along, McKell?—I seem to recall you were planning one when we met"—this last in a different tone.

Ellery sat enthroned in an armchair, both legs in their bulky casts stretched out before him, resting on a hassock. Each morning he was hoisted out of bed, and each evening he was hoisted back in. Books, magazines, tobacco, fruit, writing materials, a bottle of wine, the telephone, were within reach. There was even a remote-control device for the television set.

"I didn't come here to talk about my novel," Dane said.

"Then it can only be about your father."

Dane nodded bleakly.

"I've followed the case." Ellery glanced at both of them. "But newspaper accounts leave everything to be desired. Tell me all about it."

Dane told him everything—everything, that is, but his own attack on Sheila. When he was finished, Judy went into a detailed account of their unsuccessful search for the bar and the bartender who alone could give Ashton McKell the alibi he so desperately needed.

Ellery listened, questioned, took notes. Then he leaned back in his armchair and lost himself in thought. There was a long silence. The little noises of the hospital —the clatter of a tray, the hoarse voice of the communicator, the rattle of a dressing cart, the hum of a floor polisher . . . Ellery seemed asleep with his eyes open. Dane found himself wishing that he could sleep—for a hundred years, to wake up and find that recent events had receded into the harmless pages of history.

Suddenly Ellery said, "One question. It comes down to that."

"Of course, Mr. Queen," Judy said. "What bar was Mr. McKell in?"

"No. Strange that the question hasn't been asked before. It's the heart of the matter. The whole case may well center in it." His voice dribbled away.

Just then a glorious blond nurse came in, seemed disappointed to find company present, exchanged smiles with the patient, and hurried out. Ellery, still smiling, reached for the phone, identified himself by name and room number, and gave the hospital operator the telephone number of police headquarters.

"Inspector Queen, please . . . Dad? . . . No, I'm fine. Dad, Dane McKell is with me . . . I know, he told me. I wish you'd do something for me. I want to see his father . . . Wait a minute! There's something I must ask Mr. McKell, and you'll have to arrange it with the D.A.'s office . . . Come on, Dad, you certainly can. Today is Saturday, the trial is recessed, there's plenty of precedent . . . Yes, it's important, or I wouldn't ask you. All right? . . . I'll phone you as usual tonight."

He turned back to his visitors. "There's something wholesome to be said about old-fashioned drag. Have some fruit, you two. Or wine? McKell, about your novel . . ."

An hour and a half later he was saying, "Confound it, Dane, it doesn't matter in the slightest if the old stone quarry has fish in it or not. As long as Jerry thinks it has, it's reason enough for him to go there. So in your third chapter . . ." Someone knocked on the door. "Yes?"

And there stood Ashton McKell, between two detectives, a gray-haired one and one who looked like Sugar Ray Robinson.

The fall sun through the windows fell on the elder McKell's face, and it seemed to Dane paler and hollower even than when he had seen his father in the Tombs. There was a dream quality to the experience, standing in the sunny hospital room touching his father's shoulder while Judy clung to his free arm murmuring, "Oh, Mr. McKell," over and over in a litany of grief and pleasure, while the two detectives bantered with the man in the casts.

"Ellery, you damn fool," the gray-haired one said, "getting yourself banged up like this. You look like a goalie at the Garden."

"Floogle yourself, Piggott," Ellery said pleasantly, "and may all four of your legs never know a splint. Zillie, what are you doing out on a daytime assignment?"

The other detective grinned and said, "It's a fact the Inspector reserves me for the nighttime tricks, says I blend better with the dark." His brown wrist was locked to Ashton McKell's.

"Look, men, it's been a lovely visit," said Ellery. "Now would you wait in the hall?"

"Well," said Detective Piggott cautiously.

"You know we can't do that, Ellery," Detective Zilgitt said. "Got no business being here at all. How did you swing it?"

"Never mind how. And Piggie, don't give me any of your legalistic hawing. I'm being allowed to see Mr. McKell as a friend of the court. That makes me an officer of the court, which in turn makes what I have to say to him privileged."

"In a Piggott's eye." said Piggott. "You going to be responsible, broken legs and all?"

"I'm responsible."

"Well, just in case," Zilgitt said, "we'll be outside the door." He unlocked the handcuffs and the detectives left the room.

Ashton McKell shook hands with Ellery. "I don't know what you want to talk to me about, Mr. Queen, but I'm not looking a gift horse under the tail. It seems to me I've lived in a cell for twenty years."

"Dane, Miss Walsh, tell Mr. McKell what you two have been up to."

Dane did so. Ash McKell listened quietly; he seemed a little bewildered, as if at a new experience. "And Mr. Queen has one important question to ask you, Dad. That's why you're here."

"From the story I've been told," Ellery said, "and I assume it's the whole story, we can take for granted that the police have searched certain places thoroughly—Miss Grey's apartment, your apartment, Mr. McKell, your office and so on."

Ashton McKell looked puzzled now.

"And yet," Ellery went on, "one thing has never been mentioned. It was not, after all, Ashton McKell who called each Wednesday on Sheila Grey, was it? It was Dr. Stone. Correct? That was your invariable practice?"

The prisoner nodded slowly. Dane looked chagrined.

"Ashton McKell got into the Continental, and Dr. Stone climbed out. Somewhere between the back door of the Cricket Club and that garage off Park Avenue, Ashton McKell with the assistance of the contents of a little black bag became Dr. Stone. The question I want answered—the one that nobody seems to have thought of asking—is: *Mr. McKell, what happened to your little black bag?*"

Dane's father looked confused. "I'll have to think . . . Does it matter, Mr. Queen?"

Ellery banged on one of his casts. "Does it matter!" he cried. "Obviously the police haven't found it, or you can bet it would be one of the People's exhibits at the trial right now. There hasn't been a word about 'Dr. Stone'—no identification of the bag, no testimony about Dr. Stone's weekly visits to the Grey apartment, no identification of you as Dr. Stone, no placing of the 'doctor' on the scene of the crime, and so on. Not only haven't the police found the bag containing your make-up materials, they've never even connected you with such a bag. Seems to me it's proved the perfect disguise. Too perfect. So I repeat: What happened to the bag?"

Ashton shook his head, sank into a chair, shading his eyes.

"Take it a step at a time," Ellery said encouragingly. "You had it with you when you left the airport that night after getting off the plane from Washington?"

"Yes. I remember carrying it into Sheila's—Miss Grey's apartment. I was there such a short time. Did I . . . ? Yes, I had it when I left. I recall shifting it from one hand to the other as I walked the streets—changing hands, because I was also carrying my overnight bag. And I had it with me in that bar. I know, because I recall setting it down on the bar stool beside me."

"Do you remember taking it home with you, Mr. McKell?"

"I didn't have it when I got home. I'm sure of that. Could I have left it in the bar? No . . . I recall picking it up as I left the bar . . . I wouldn't have taken it home. Usually I kept it locked up in my room at the Cricket. But I was closer to Grand Central at the time—"

"Grand Central," Ellery said softly.

Ashton was looking astonished. "I did say Grand Central, didn't I? How our minds play tricks on us! That's it, of course. I checked it at the baggage room, or whatever it's called—the counter. When I left the bar I must have walked all the way down to Grand Central. And I didn't remember it!"

"Where is the baggage check, Mr. McKell?"

"Probably still in the suit I wore the night I got home."

Dane said slowly, "Then how is it the police didn't find it when they searched your things?"

"Never mind that now, Dane," Ellery said briskly. "Get on this phone and call your mother. Have her look for it at once."

It was the senior maid, old Margaret, who answered.

"But I can't call Mrs. McKell," Margaret protested. "Herself says I'm not to disturb her for *no* reason, Mr. Dane, not a single one." It seemed that his mother had

85

locked the door in the corridor leading to her separate apartment—bedroom, bath, sitting room—with the strictest instructions. Meals were to be left on a wagon at the door. She would not see anyone, and she would not answer the telephone.

"Maggie, listen to me. Did you find anything in my father's rooms the morning we got the news about Miss Grey? Or afterward? Did you find . . . ?"

He was about to say "a tan suit," but old Margaret interrupted him. "The phone, Mr. Dane," came her Irish whisper. "Maybe it's tapped." Dane was dumfounded. The possibility had not occurred to him. Could it be that Margaret knew about the suit, *had* found the baggage check?

To his further surprise, Margaret uttered three more words and hung up on him. He put the receiver down foolishly.

"Mother won't talk on the phone and Margaret's afraid it may be tapped. But I think she knows. She said to me, 'Go to Bridey,' and hung up. Dad, who the deuce is Bridey?"

"It's her younger sister, Bridget Donnelly. Her husband used to work for me."

"But I don't understand."

"You don't have to understand, Dane," said Judy. "You go and do as old Maggie says. Find Bridey."

"Miss Walsh is right," said Ellery. "And do it fast, Dane. I don't know how long I can bluff that pair out there into letting me keep custody of your father."

Ramon drove him over to Chelsea in the Bentley. Mrs. Donnelly lived in a crumble-edged brownstone, in a musty but spotless apartment. She was a stouter version of her sister Margaret. "You *say* you'll be Mister Dane McKell?" she demanded as she showed him into a parlor decorated with lithochromes of St. Lawrence O'Toole and the Sacred Heart. "And how would I be knowing that?"

It had not occurred to him that he would require

identification. "Look, Mrs. Donnelly, I'm in an awful hurry." He explained his mission.

But Bridey Donnelly was not to be rushed.

"You called up me sister Margaret," she said, "and you asked her about something important for your father, may the saints deliver him from harm; ain't I been praying for him night and day?—and Maggie said, 'Go to Bridey,' and you think that means she give it to me. Well, and what might it be you think she give to me, Mr. Dane McKell-Maybe-You-Are-and-Maybe-You-Ain't?"

Her concern over his father was plainly not going to get in the way of her Irish caution. "Tan suit?" Dane said.

She shook her head. "Don't know what you're talking about."

"Claim check? Baggage? Grand Central?"

"Still don't. Keep talking."

By this time he could have throttled her. "A black bag, then."

The words were no sooner out of his mouth than she waddled off, beckoning him to follow. Down past the dark chain of bedrooms in the railroad flat she plodded, and stopped in the last but one, where she switched on the light. The little bedroom mirror was still decorated with desiccated fronds from Palm Sunday seven months before.

"You're younger than me, and a lot skinnier," Bridget Donnelly said. "You get it. 'Tis under the bed."

The only thing he could find under the bed was an ancient horsehair trunk with an Ould Sod look. He dragged it out. "But it's locked."

She rapped him on the forehead with her knuckles as he turned his head. "You look the other way a minute now," directed Mrs. Donnelly, "for all you're a boy and I'm an old widow woman." Petticoats rustled. "Here." She thrust a trunk key, fastened to a safety pin, over his shoulder. He got the trunk open, flung back the lid. "Leave me do it," the widow said, taking out a Douay Bible that must have weighed twenty pounds. Under the Bible lay a tightly packed wad of clothing. And under the clothing there was a black leather bag.

He got to his feet, stammering his thanks.

"And you can save your thanks, young man. We know whose bread and salt we've et these thirty years, Maggie and me and me dead Tom. And now go on about your business, and let me hear over the radio that your blessed father's okay."

Dane kissed her. She boxed his ear, grinning. It rang halfway back to the hospital.

He had been gone less than forty minutes. The detectives in the corridor glanced at the bag he was carrying, but neither of them said anything, and he went into Ellery's room with a sigh of relief.

Ellery's silvery eyes lighted up at sight of the bag. "Good for you, Dane! All right, Mr. McKell."

Dane's father opened the bag and quickly set its contents on Ellery's dresser. He began to apply grease paint and spirit gum to his face.

"What the devil?"

Ellery chuckled at Dane's cry. He glanced at Judy, but that young lady was busy with a small camera, adjusting a flash bulb.

"Let me sum it up for you, Dane," said Ellery. "You, Judy and the police have been searching for the wrong man. Of course no one in any of those bars recognized Ashton McKell. He wasn't Ashton McKell that night. He was Dr. Stone."

Ashton began to pluck at a bundle of gray fibers. He arranged them on his chin in Vandyke fashion, working with the sureness of long practice.

"What a chump I've been," Dane groaned. "That's what comes of trying to play detective. Dad, where did you make the change that night?"

"In one of the men's rooms at the airport when I got off the plane," replied his father. "Then after I left Sheila's and wandered off, eventually winding up at Grand Central, I removed the make-up in the Grand Central men's room, although I didn't bother to change out of the tan suit. Then I checked the black bag and went home. It's all come back. Mr. Queen's acted as a sort of oxygen tent. The fresh air's cleared the cobwebs out of my head."

When he turned from the mirror Ashton McKell was no longer Ashton McKell but gray-haired, gray-bearded Dr. Stone. It was remarkable how the false hair and the really skillful touches he had applied to his eyes and face transformed his appearance.

Judy sat him down and circled him with her camera, searching for the best angle. The bulb flashed, Judy said, "One or two more, just to be sure," she took a second shot, then a profile, and then said, "Come back, Mr. McKell—I feel *funny* looking at you," and Ashton McKell even laughed as he removed the false hair and make-up and became himself again. But then they heard him mutter, "How did I ever get mixed up in this foolishness?"

"The classic question, Mr. McKell," Ellery remarked dryly. " '*Oh, what a tangled web we weave,*' and so on. Are we ready? Call them in, Dane."

When the detectives had departed with their prisoner, Ellery waved cheerfully. "Now, you two. The pubs await you. Start crawling. Meanwhile, I'll phone Bob O'Brien and see if I can get him to talk Judge Suarez and the D.A. into agreeing to a forty-eight-hour recess —even a twenty-four-hour stay may do it. I think we can get it. O'Brien can do more things with his tongue than the head chef at the Waldorf."

When they were gone, Ellery leaned over and rang for the nurse. He seemed pleased with himself.

"I'm worn down," he said to the ravishing blonde when she came in, "and I badly need tuning up. Put on a record, Kirsten, skin me a grape, and tell me you're not going to be busy the night of the day they finally peel off these plaster pants."

"Pardon?" said the girl, frowning.

"This armchair Hawkshaw role is debilitating. What price Mycroft Holmes?"

"Mr. Queen, I do not understand—"

"Never mind, Kirsten. Teach me your native tongue. All I know is *akavit* and *snoose*. Meanwhile, I'll try not to let your Nordic beauty overexcite me. May I hold your hand?"

The nurse gave him her sizzling smile. "I think you are very yoking, Mr. Queen. But it is nice yoke, no?"

"It is nice yoke, yes. Would you hand me the phone?"

On the morning the trial resumed there was a marked alteration of the atmosphere. No cluster of bankers, non-career ambassadors, bishops, and captains of industry waited to take the stand. Robert O'Brien arose, in a radiation of confidence. Something not quite a whisper or ripple passed through the courtroom and reached His Honor, who looked up from the bench sharply. The judge, grown so old in the juridical service that he had developed a sixth sense, felt his sleepiness slip away and that telltale tingle in his brain that made him sit up in his swivel chair.

Bob O'Brien was in his early forties, a burly Irishman with the face of a boy. He specialized in lost legal causes and brought them off with amazing consistency. A family man, a Harvard man, learned in history and the classics, he was a Sunday painter, a summer archeologist, and a courtroom terror. He had just fought a penniless defendant's murder case through three mistrials to an acquittal. His successful defense of an alien from deportation earned him the sobriquet of "the new Darrow" in liberal circles; then when he sued for the right of a handicapped child to obtain special transportation to a parochial school on public funds, he lost the most vocal part of his support.

Bob O'Brien, then, on that November morning, rose.

"Call Ashton McKell," he said, to the tune of another murmur. McKell, chin high, took the stand as if it were the chair at an international shippers' convention, and the oath as if it admitted him to clerical orders.

"State your full name."

"Philip Cornelius Ashton McKell."

"Have you ever used another name?"

"Yes."

District Attorney De Angelus leaned forward as if impelled by a wire.

"What name was that?"

"Dr. Stone."

The D.A. shook his head as if to dislodge something from his ear.

"This other name—Dr. Stone—was it an alias?"

"No."

"Please explain just what use you put it to, Mr. McKell."

"It involved an entirely different identity. In order to become Dr. Stone, I would put on make-up and clothing of a type I do not ordinarily wear. I also used false eyeglasses, which I do not need to see by, and carried a walking stick and a physician's black bag."

"All this in your Dr. Stone identity?"

"Yes."

Bob O'Brien was back at his table and reaching under it. He pulled out the little satchel. "Is this the bag you refer to, Mr. McKell?"

"It is."

"Would you open it and display its contents?"

Ashton McKell did so. "This is spirit gum, this is false gray hair, this is . . ."

"In other words, Mr. McKell, this bag contains make-up materials for a disguise?"

"Yes, except for the clothing and cane."

"Thank you. I place this bag and its contents in evidence as defendant's Exhibit—"

The judge opened his mouth, but too slowly. District Attorney De Angelus was finally on his feet, waving wildly.

"Your Honor, may I ask Counsel what is the relevance of this evidence?"

"It is necessary for my client," said O'Brien, "to use the contents of this bag in order to make himself up."

"In this courtroom?" cried the district attorney.

"In this courtroom," said the Irishman courteously.

"Here? Now?"

"Here and now."

"Counsel," said His Honor, "we all appreciate the more colorful practices you occasionally indulge in in the courtroom—when you're permitted to get away with them—but tell me: What is the purpose of introducing amateur theatricals into this trial?"

O'Brien permitted himself to look disconcerted. "I

hadn't intended to reveal defense's reasons so early. However, if Your Honor insists—"

"His Honor insists," said His Honor.

"Very well, Mr. McKell, will you tell the Court, please, for what purpose you were accustomed to assuming this false identity?"

"In order to conceal my true identity." Ash McKell hesitated for the briefest moment. "I mean while visiting the apartment of Miss Sheila Grey."

"Order! Counsel will approach the bench. You, too, Mr. District Attorney."

There was a three-cornered whispered conversation of considerable liveliness before the bench. Finally De Angelus waved his hand wearily. Judge Suarez said, "The exhibit will be admitted," and everybody sat down but a bailiff who moved a small table to a position before the witness chair, set the black bag on it, and retired. McKell removed the contents of the bag, which included a small swivel-mirror on a stand, and spread them on the table.

"Mr. McKell," said Bob O'Brien, as if he were ordering a ham sandwich on rye, "make yourself up as Dr. Stone."

And Ashton McKell, eighty to a hundred times a millionaire, adviser of Presidents, refuser of ambassadorships, proceeding to make himself up in full fascinated view of judge, jury, prosecutor, defense counsel, bailiffs, the press, and spectators.

When the tycoon was Dr. Stone, he straightened up from the mirror and glanced at his lawyer. The silence hung, broke. The gavel rapped, and the silence hung again.

O'Brien: "And this is how you always looked when you posed as Dr. Stone?"

"Yes, except for the tan suit and walking stick."

"I think we can imagine those. All right, Mr. McKell. Your Honor, in the interest of more orderly development, I should like Mr. McKell's testimony to be interrupted while we introduce the testimony of two other witnesses. If the Court and the district attorney don't object?"

Another colloquy. McKell was told to stand down, and O'Brien said, "Call John Leslie."

Leslie, shaven to a violent pink, stiff in the same suit he had worn to stand on the sidewalk and cheer the visiting Queen Elizabeth and Prince Philip, was called into the courtroom and sworn, and he testified that he was the doorman of 610½ Park Avenue, and had been since it opened its doors as a multiple dwelling. He had therefore known Mr. Ashton McKell, yes, sir, for over twenty-five years.

"Do you see Mr. McKell in this courtroom?"

Leslie scanned the room. He looked puzzled. "No, sir, I do not."

"Well, would you recognize a Dr. Stone?" asked O'Brien.

"Dr. Stone? You mean the doctor who used to visit Miss Grey? I think so, sir."

"Do you see Dr. Stone in this courtroom?"

Leslie looked around. "Yes, sir."

"Point him out, please . . . Thank you, Mr. Leslie. That's all."

District Attorney De Angelus: "Mr. Leslie, do you recall the night Miss Grey's body was found?"

"Yes, sir."

"On that night, did this man you have identified as Dr. Stone visit the apartment building at 610½ Park?"

"Yes, sir."

"At what time?"

"It was quite late in the evening. Somewhere around ten o'clock."

"Can you be more exact as to the time?"

"No, sir. I had no reason to."

"Do you recall his leaving the building?"

"Yes, sir, not long after. A few minutes. I wasn't paying much attention."

"A half hour?"

"Might be."

"You just said a few minutes."

"I just don't know, sir."

"That's all."

Surprisingly, O'Brien did not recross. "I call Ramon Alvarez."

Old John departed, still frowning over the incomprehensibility of the proceedings, to be succeeded on the stand by Ramon. Who testified that he had been employed as Ashton McKell's chauffeur for the past five years; that since early spring—about April, he thought it was—he had at his employer's direction been driving him, Ashton McKell, in the Bentley, at about four o'clock each Wednesday afternoon, to the front door of the Metropolitan Cricket Club. It was his, Ramon's, practice then to park the Bentley at a garage behind the club.

"What did you do then?"

"I would have orders to meet Mr. McKell back at the club late that night, with the Bentley."

"Did Mr. McKell ever tell you where he was going on those Wednesday evenings?"

"No, sir."

"This happened *every* Wednesday since about April, Mr. Alvarez?"

"Once or twice not, when Mr. McKell was in South America or Europe, on business."

O'Brien turned. "Mr. McKell, would you stand up? Thank you. Mr. Alvarez, did you ever see Mr. McKell dressed and made up as he appears right now?"

"Sir, no."

"You're sure of that."

"Sir, yes."

"You were never curious as to where Mr. McKell was going on Wednesday nights?" O'Brien persisted. "Without you to drive him?"

Ramon shrugged. "I am the chauffeur, sir. I do what I am told."

"And not once did you see him in make-up . . . ?"

"Your Honor," said the district attorney, "Mr. O'Brien is cross-examining his own witness."

O'Brien waved, De Angelus waved, and Ramon was dismissed.

"I recall Ashton McKell to the stand." When Ashton resumed the witness box, being admonished that he was still under oath, O'Brien said, "Mr. McKell, I am going to ask you a painful question. What was your underlying reason for disguising yourself each Wednesday as a non-existent Dr. Stone—even going so far as to conceal the disguise from your own chauffeur?"

"I didn't want my family or anyone else to know about my visits to Miss Grey." The courtroom rustled.

"In this," added the elder McKell bitterly, "I seem to have failed with a bang."

It was an unfortunate metaphor. Someone in the courtroom tittered, and at least one newspaper reporter dodged out to phone his paper the "expert psychiatric opinion" that the *lapsus linguae* might well have been a Freudian slip by which the accused confessed his guilt. As for O'Brien, he frowned ever so slightly; he did not care for witnesses who volunteered information on the stand, especially defendants. He was taken off the hook by the district attorney, who had not caught the inference and was fretting about the accused's sitting around the courtroom like an actor at a dress rehearsal. He said so, emphatically.

"The defendant will remain in make-up only a little while longer, Your Honor," O'Brien said, "and only for the purpose of having one other witness corroborate his identity."

Judge Suarez waved, and O'Brien went on: "I will ask you to tell us once again, Mr. McKell, of your arrival at Miss Grey's apartment on the night of September 14th, and of what happened subsequently." He led Ashton through his story. "Then you don't remember the name of the bar? Or where it was located?"

"I do not."

"Your witness."

De Angelus's cross-examination was long, detailed, theatrical, and futile. He could not shake the defendant's story, although he spattered it liberally with the mud of doubt. In the end McKell sat labeled adulterer, home-wrecker, betrayer of trust in high places, perverted aristocrat, corrupt citizen of the democracy, and above all murderer. It was an artistic job, and it made Dane and Judy writhe; but no flicker of anger or resentment—or shame—touched the elder McKell's stone-hard face; and Robert O'Brien simply listened with his big head cocked, boyishly attentive, even—one would have thought—a little pleased.

When the district attorney sat down, sated, O'Brien idly said, "Call Matthew Thomas Cleary to the stand."

A thick-set man with curly gray hair was sworn. He had a squashed nose and round blue eyes that seemed to say: We have seen everything, and nothing matters. His brogue was refreshing, delivered in a hoarse voice.

He was Matthew Thomas Cleary, part owner and sometime bartender of the Kerry Dancers Bar and Grill on 59th Street off First Avenue. He had never been in trouble with the law, saints be praised.

"Now, Mr. Cleary," O'Brien said easily, walking over to "Dr. Stone" and touching his shoulder, "have you ever seen this man before?"

"Yes, sor. In me bar one night."

O'Brien strolled back to the witness stand. "You're sure, Mr. Cleary? You couldn't be mistaken?"

"That I could not."

A police officer escorted a woman to a seat at the rear of the courtroom, unnoticed. Her face under the half-veil was chalky. It was Lutetia McKell, sucked out of her shell at last.

"Mr. Cleary, you must see hundreds of faces across your bar. What makes you remember this man's face?"

" 'Twas this way, sor. He was wearing this beard. That was in the first place. The Kerry Dancers bar don't get one customer in a thousand wears a beard. So that makes him stick in me mind. Second place, on the shelf behind the bar I got me a big jar with a sign on it, 'The Children of Loretto,' that's this orphanage out on Staten Island. I put the small change into it that people leave on the bar. This fellow with the beard, his first drink he gives me a twenty, I give him change, and he shoves over a five-dollar bill. 'Put that in the jar,' he says, 'for the orphan children.' And I did, and I thanked him. *That* makes me remember him. Nobody else ever give me a five-dollar bill for the jar."

"What night was this, Mr. Cleary?" O'Brien asked suddenly.

"September 14th, sor."

"You mean to say, Mr. Cleary, you can remember the exact night two months ago that this man had a drink at your bar and gave you a five-dollar bill for The Children of Loretto?"

"Yes, sor. On account of that was the night of the championship fight. I'd drew a ring around the date on me bar calendar so I wouldn't forget, I mean so I'd remember not to turn on a movie or a speech or something on the bar TV instead of the fights. And this man come in, like I say—"

District Attorney De Angelus was sitting on the edge of the chair at his table, elbows planted securely, listening with both cocked ears in a kind of philosophic panic.

"Let's not go too fast, Mr. Cleary. All right, it was the night of the championship prize fight, September 14th, and that made you remember the date. But how can you be so sure this man with the beard came in on *that* night? Couldn't it have been on some other night?"

"No, *sor*," said Cleary stoutly. "On account of him and me was talking about the fight. I says, 'Time for the big fight any minute now,' and he says, 'Big fight?' like he never heard of the fights. 'Who's fighting?' he says— a championship fight! So I tell him the champ is battling this Puerto Rican challenger, Kid Aguirre, and he looks at me like I'm talking Siwash."

"And that made you remember it was this man, on that particular night?"

"Wouldn't it make anybody? Anyways, I turn on the TV and we watch the fight. After the first round I says to him—"

"To the gentleman with the gray beard?"

"Sure, who else we talking about? I says to him, 'What d'ye think?' And he says, 'That boy—the Kid— he'll never make it. He ain't got what it takes. The champ will knock him out,' he says to me."

"One moment, Mr. Cleary. Mr. McKell, will you please rise—it isn't necessary to come forward—and face this witness? Now will you please say in a conversational tone, 'That boy will never make it. The champ will knock him out.' "

"That boy will never make it," said Ashton McKell. "The champ will knock him out."

"Mr. Cleary, to the best of your recollection, is that the voice, the same voice, of the gray-bearded man you talked to in your bar on the night of September 14th?"

"Sure and it's the same, ain't that what I'm telling you, sor?"

"You're sure it's the same voice."

"I can hear it ringing in me ears," said Cleary poetically, "right now."

O'Brien quickened the pace of his questions. They

97

watched the fight, Cleary said, and in round two they made a ten-dollar bet on the outcome, Cleary maintaining that Kid Aguirre would last the full fifteen rounds, the gray-bearded man insisting that the Kid would be knocked out. And knocked out he was, "as ye'll remember, sor, in the third, to me sorrow."

"Did you pay the man the ten dollars?"

"He wouldn't let me. 'Put it in the jar for the orphans,' he says, which I done."

"One last question, Mr. Cleary: You and this gray-haired man were watching the original telecast of the fight, not a rerun on tape?"

Cleary was sure. The fight had been fought in Denver over closed-circuit television, but it was telecast live for the East, and the tapes were not shown anywhere until the following day.

The district attorney made a savage attempt to break down Cleary's identification of "Dr. Stone." But luck had thrown a stubborn Irishman his way. The harder De Angelus hammered, the more positive Cleary became. When the cross-examination became abusive, O'Brien politely stepped in: "It seems to me, Your Honor, the witness has answered each of the district attorney's questions not once but half a dozen times. I think we are approaching the point of badgering, and I respectfully call your attention to it."

The judge glared at O'Brien, but he stopped De Angelus.

Nothing was left for O'Brien but to thrust the point between the horns. He introduced into evidence the official time of the Kid Aguirre knockout, as certified by the timekeeper of the championship fight and the records of the Colorado boxing commission.

Time of knockout: 10:27:46—forty-six seconds after twenty-seven minutes after ten o'clock P.M. Eastern Time.

Robert O'Brien summed up for the defense: "I am sure it isn't necessary, ladies and gentlemen of the jury, to remind you that none of us is here in this courtroom to punish moral turpitude. The question you are asked to decide is not one of sin but of guilt. There is only one question on which His Honor will charge you to consider your verdict, and that is: Was the defendant, Ashton McKell, guilty of murdering Sheila Grey by gunshot at twenty-three minutes past ten o'clock on the night of September 14th? You have heard testimony here that must convince anyone that Mr. McKell could not physically have been guilty of that crime. He could not have committed it because, at the time it was committed, he was seated at a bar half a city mile from the scene of the crime, and continued to sit there for some time afterward.

"Not only could Ashton McKell not have shot Sheila Grey, he could not have been at or even near the scene of her death when the fatal shot was fired.

"I repeat: No other aspect of the case should concern you, or—under what I am confident will be Judge Suarez's charge—legally can concern you. Consequently, no reasonable man or woman could bring in a verdict of anything but not guilty."

The waiting was a stasis, the blood piling up in the vessel to the bursting point, the question being would there be resolution and relief before the complete blockage and eruption. Reporters spotted Lutetia McKell and crowded round her, to her distress, until Richard M. Heaton rescued her; none of them dared leave the courtroom while the jury deliberated; they sat and talked, or were mute, thinking their own thoughts. Heaton tended to be optimistic, O'Brien noncommittal ("I never speculate on what a jury will or will not do"), except to point out that District Attorney De Angelus had not left the room, indicating the prosecution's belief that the jury would not be out long—for whatever that was worth; De Angelus himself was the recipient of a message, delivered to him by messenger, to which he dashed of an immediate reply, and sank back only to be aroused by another messenger with another envelope.

"He's kept so very busy, isn't he?" said Lutetia. Then she began nibbling at her handkerchief.

So Dane and Judy captured her attention by telling the story of their original unsuccessful search for the bar and bartender, and of their visit to Ellery Queen.

"That's his father, Inspector Queen, who just came and spoke to the D.A.," Robert O'Brien pointed ou

And of the lightning development of the hunt ther after.

Lutetia was touched. "Margaret is so faithful," sl said. "You know, Dane, how she worships your father. suppose all along she's known a great deal more tha any of us, from this and that picked up at random. Sl must have realized something was wrong when sl found that outlandish tan suit in Ashton's bedroom. Sl always empties the pockets of his suits, you know."

For want of something better to do, they discusse old Margaret's incredible enterprise in the matter of tl baggage claim check and the black bag. They agree that she must have found the claim check in the tan su shortly after the first visit of the police; to old Maggi Irish-born, to whom "police" and "rebel-hunters" wou forever be synonymous, at the same time loyal unt death to Ashton McKell, the sight of the claim chec must have triggered her instinct for trouble, and she ha simply secreted it to keep it out of the hands of the lav After Ashton's arrest she had sneaked down to Gran Central, found all her fears confirmed when, in retu for the check, she was handed the little black bag, an promptly enlisted her sister as a confederate, hiding tl bag in her sister's flat for no other reason than to keep from being found by the authorities, who were searchir everything pertaining to McKell.

"Hers not to reason why," said Dane. "Good o Maggie."

"Something's about to break," said O'Brien alertl "Look at what's going on at the D.A.'s table . . . was right. There goes the bailiff into the judge's chamber The jury's probably reached a verdict."

They had.

Not guilty.

There was a frantic moment when everyone was in mc tion—hands clasping, lips babbling, backs being slappec Ashton embracing Lutetia (in public!), Dane embracin

Judy (both electrically surprised at the naturalness with which they turned and fell into each other's arms)— then everything suddenly stopped, hands, eyes, mouths, everything. For an instant it was hard to say why, because really nothing had happened except the approach of a very large man grasping a folded piece of paper. But then it came through: there was something in his very approach, a balls-of-the-feet guardedness, the way his great fingers grasped the paper, the hard look on his hard face, that was like a gush of ice water.

It was Sergeant Velie.

Who said politely, "Mr. McKell."

Ashton still had his arm about Lutetia. "Yes?"

"If you don't mind, sir," Sergeant Velie said, "I have to speak to Mrs. McKell."

"To my *wife?*"

It seemed to Dane that his mother started and then took a perceptible grip on herself.

But her glance at the big sergeant was coldly courteous. "Yes? What is it, please?"

"I'm going to have to ask you," said the detective, "to come down to police headquarters with me."

Lutetia stirred, ever so slightly. Her husband blinked. Dane moved forward angrily: "What's this all about, Sergeant? Why do you want to take my mother—of all people!—down to headquarters?"

"Because I have to book her," the sergeant said impassively, "on a charge of suspicion of the murder of Sheila Grey."

III. The Third Side

LUTETIA

There was confusion. Dane kept running around looking for the lawyers, who had left the courtroom. Ashton interposed his formidable body between his wife and the sergeant as if he expected an assault. Judy looked about wildly for Dane. Reporters, catching the drama, were beginning to converge on the group with everything flapping. The sergeant said, "I have to ask you to step out of the way, Mr. McKell. This'll turn into a mob scene if you don't let me get her out of here quick."

Detective Mack had materialized; he was reaching around Ashton to get at Lutetia.

Somehow they managed to shoulder their way through the shouting newsmen.

"I'm sorry, Sergeant," growled Ashton, "but we're going down to headquarters all together."

"You can't do that, Mr. McKell."

"Can't we?"

"There isn't room in the car—"

"There is in mine."

"Look, men," roared the sergeant, "you'll get your stories later. Mack, hold these croakers off, will you? Let us through!"

"Where's Dane?"

"Here he is, Mr. McKell!" Judy screamed.

"They'd already left the building." Dane elbowed his way through. "I've phoned their offices."

"Get out of the way, will you?"

They drove up to police headquarters from the courthouse in the McKell Continental, Velie trying visibly to smooth his feathers. In the lobby he said to the McKells and Judy, "I'm sorry, but you people will have to wait here."

"Either we all go," Ashton retorted, "or we all wait until my lawyers get here."

"That's not the way we do things, Mr. McKell. Your wife is under arrest—"

Lutetia was standing beside her husband, turned to stone down to the marbled fingers clutching his arm. Dane thought she was going to faint, and he jumped for-

103

ward to support her on the other side; but she did no
He thought: She's pretending she isn't here, that this
all a bad dream. He was not surprised to see her sh
her eyes like a child. Then he felt himself shoulders
aside by Judy, who slipped her hand into the old
woman's, squeezing it, murmuring something. But L
tetia did not respond.

"Mr. McKell, you going to stand aside?" bellowed th
sergeant.

"I am not," said Ashton. "I know of no state or mu
nicipal law forbidding the family and attorneys of an a
rested person to be present during the preliminary que
tioning by the authorities. Unless you allow it, Sergean
I'm going to insist that my wife be taken before a magi
trate at once—you know as well as I that that's her rig
until she's formally charged. Meanwhile, please let
have some place to sit down."

Sergeant Velie muttered, "*Okay*. Come on," and the
trooped after him and into Inspector Queen's offic
where he engaged in some hasty, red-eared, whispere
explanations. Meanwhile, Ashton handed his wife into
comfortable chair and said to Dane, "Better tell Ramo
where we are, so he can tell O'Brien and Heaton whe
they get here."

Dane hurried back downstairs. When he returned, h
found Inspector Queen talking quietly to Lutetia, wit
Sergeant Velie standing stormily by. It seemed that As
ton had made a dicker with the Inspector; in return fo
being allowed to be present during Lutetia's preliminar
questioning, Ashton had agreed not to insist on waitin
for the lawyers. Inspector Queen seemed in comple
charge of the case now. This, then, was why he had vi
ited the courtroom, what all the whispering and mes
sages at the district attorney's table had been abou

But why was his mother being held in the murder fo
which his father had just been acquitted? Dane straine
to find out.

"Mrs. McKell, this is as painful to me as it is to you,
the Inspector was saying. "All you have to do is answe
some questions to my satisfaction, and that will be that.

"Whatever I can," Lutetia whispered. Her tiny hand
were clasped about her purse as if it were holding he
instead of the other way around.

"And if you want anything, just say so and I'll have a matron called."

"Thank you."

He began.

Her answers tended to be erratic, as if she were not putting her whole mind into the interrogation. Yes, she remembered the night of September 14th. She had had dinner delayed in the hope that her husband might have decided to return home from Washington instead of staying overnight. (Did the merest flush come into her cheeks?) After dinner she had gone to the music room and tried to read. She had dismissed the servants for the night—they all slept out.

"But I found I couldn't concentrate on Mrs. Oliphant's novel," Lutetia said. "So I thought I would catch up on my needlework . . ." She wandered off into reminiscence. "It reminds me of when I was a girl. I tended to be willful, especially about things like needlework, and my grandmother was quite severe with me about it. 'When *I* was a girl,' she would say, 'I had to learn spinning and weaving as well.' I remember when she lay dying. It all came back to her. I suppose she confused me with her sister, after whom I am named, because she said to me, 'Lutetia, have you carded the flax yet?' Of course I said, 'Yes, dear.' And it seemed to me she looked pleased. She said to me then, 'Whatsoever thy hands find to do, do it with all thy might.'"

Dane thought: Damn your girlhood reflections, Mother! You'll hang yourself.

Inspector Queen had listened patiently. Whether he found Lutetia's reminiscence of special interest Dane could not tell. The old man waited for a moment, then he cleared his throat. "How long did you spend on your needlework that evening, Mrs. McKell? Can you recall?"

She looked surprised. "I didn't spend any time at all on my needlework. I said I only thought about doing so."

"You did, didn't you? Excuse me, Mrs. McKell, I guess I wasn't paying close enough attention. Then you didn't do any sewing that night. What did you do?—after putting the book down, I mean?"

Astonishingly, Lutetia uttered the ghost of a giggle.

Inspector Queen looked dumfounded. It was as if Queen Victoria had belched.

"I'm ashamed to say, Inspector. Well, I suppose it can't be helped. Oh, dear, now you'll think me a complete scatterbrain. Dane, you remember I told you when you came in just past midnight—"

The Inspector glanced at Dane.

"Mother was watching television," Dane said curtly. He was embarrassed. Why did she have to be such a prig? The old policeman would think it was an act. How could he believe she was being herself? How could anyone who didn't know her?

"Well, we won't make a federal case out of *that*," Inspector Queen said dryly. "It's a vice shared by a lot of people, they tell me. Mrs. McKell, how long did you watch TV?"

"For almost *three* hours," Lutetia confessed.

"Do you remember what you saw?"

"Oh . . . dear. I'm afraid I can't. They're all sort of the same, aren't they? I do recall some old motion picture . . ."

The Inspector pressed her softly. He got little out of her. She had not left the apartment, she had had no visitors.

"We don't seem to be getting anywhere," the old gentleman remarked at last.

"Because there's no place to get." Ashton McKell rose. "My wife stayed home, Inspector. How can she remember the details of an evening in which nothing happened, and during which she was alone? On what ground are you questioning her? Why are you holding her?"

"Sit down, Mr. McKell," said Inspector Queen. "This is not a desperate detention—we would hardly take a step like this without a basis in hard fact. Will you sit down? Please?"

Ashton sat down.

"Let's begin with the fundamentals again—motive, opportunity, means. I hate to poke around old sores, but Mrs. McKell certainly had motive against Sheila Grey, in view of the circumstances—the woman her husband was seeing on the sly." Ashton reddened; Lutetia reached over and patted his hand, turning him redder.

"She also had opportunity, very good opportunity—living in the same building, able to get up to the penthouse any time she wanted without being spotted, and by her own admission just now, all alone all evening until after midnight, when your son came home. There are only four apartments in the building—the Clementses are on a cruise, no one is occupying the Dill apartment at present, Mr. Dill's will being contested, with the apartment one of the assets his heirs are wrangling about. And the elevator is self-service.

"As for means." The Inspector paused. "Ordinarily I wouldn't tell you this, Mr. McKell, but considering that you were acquitted today in the same case, you people are entitled to know just why we've made this arrest. You see, today we found new evidence."

"Evidence?" Dane echoed. "What evidence?"

The old man took from the bowels of his desk a dainty lace handkerchief, bunched together as if it were wrapped around something. The monogram in the corner lay exposed.

"ALDeWMcK," he said, pointing to it. "It would be a pretty remarkable coincidence if anybody else in any way involved with Sheila Grey had this monogram. Anyway, there won't be any trouble identifying the handkerchief. This is your property, Mrs. McKell, isn't it?"

She swallowed and nodded.

The Inspector opened the handkerchief as if it held some sacred relic. Inside nestled five brass-cased .38 cartridges.

Aston McKell gaped at them. "Where did you find those?"

"In the same place as the handkerchief—in the bottom of a dressing-table drawer in your wife's dressing room. We did it legally," he added gently, "with a search warrant." Yes, thought Dane, and you did it damned fast—after that bartender's testimony gave you some second thoughts. "Along with the handkerchief and these five cartridges," and Inspector Queen reached into his drawer again and brought out a small box, "we found this ammo box, which according to the label should contain twenty .38 cartridges. Do you want to count how many are in the box?" He removed the lid;

some were missing. "I'll save you the trouble. It contains fifteen cartridges.

"But the five missing cartridges," the Inspector went on, "are not the five cartridges we found wrapped up in the handkerchief. The missing ones, like these left in the box, were live ammunition. These five in the handkerchief are blanks."

"What?" Ashton said feebly.

"Miss Grey was killed with a Smith and Wesson .38 Terrier revolver. An S. & W. .38 Terrier holds only five bullets.— Were you going to say something, Mr. McKell?"

"Are you trying to tell us," the elder McKell asked out of stiff lips, "that the five blanks in that handkerchief are the same blanks I put into the revolver?"

"Exactly. Somebody removed the five blanks you put into the gun and substituted five live shells—the five missing from this box. And the question is: Who was that somebody?"

There was a long pause. Lutetia's eyes were shut again. Judy's lips had turned pearly. In the silence the old clock on the Inspector's wall ticked noisily.

Finally Inspector Queen asked in a very kind voice, "Would you care to answer that question, Mrs. McKell?"

Lutetia opened her eyes. Her little tongue-tip flicked into view and vanished.

Ashton said hoarsely, "Don't answer another question, Lu. Not one more!"

But Lutetia said, "Why, no, Inspector Queen, I . . . don't know that I can."

It was a painful moment. Dane wished he were a thousand miles away. Judy seemed about to be sick. Ashton's hand groped for his wife's and engulfed it.

"Motive," said the Inspector. "Opportunity. No alibi. And here are the means. You'll recall we took a set of everyone's fingerprints for comparison purposes after your arrest, Mr. McKell. So we had Mrs. McKell's on file. Well, right after we found these blanks today, we examined them for prints. We found a partial print of Mrs. McKell's right forefinger and thumb on the jackets of three of these five blanks. And nobody else's. That means that you, Mrs. McKell, and you alone, handled those blanks. You removed them from the gun that subsequently killed Miss Grey."

Lutetia nodded a very little, like an old woman in her dotage. Even the Inspector seemed to realize that it was not a nod of acquiescence so much as an uncontrollable tremor.

"Hold on," said Ashton McKell hoarsely. "Did you find any fingerprints on the cases of the live shells in the gun at the time Sheila Grey's body was found?"

"We did," Inspector Queen replied, "and if the D.A. knew I'd told you that I'd face departmental charges. Well, I've stuck my neck out before. I suppose I want you people to know we're not making wild charges out of pique. Yes, we found unmistakable prints of Mrs. McKell's fingers on two of the five live cartridges. Now you know what this is all about. You, you alone, Mrs. McKell, substituted the live shells for the blank ones in the gun that killed Sheila Grey. You, and you alone, Mrs. McKell, turned that harmless gun into a murder weapon. I wouldn't be doing my job if I didn't come to the conclusion that you did so for the purpose of committing murder with it.

"So let's try it again, Mrs. McKell. Do you have anything to tell me?"

"No, you don't!" shouted Ashton. He actually clapped his hand over his wife's mouth. "Don't breathe another syllable, Lu! You don't have to say a word till you've had a chance to talk to O'Brien. That's my wife's right, Inspector!"

"It certainly is." The old policeman was on his feet now. "But I'm going to ask you one more question anyway. Mrs. McKell, did you shoot Sheila Grey to death?"

"She's not going to answer," Ashton said furiously.

The Inspector shrugged. "Get the wheels rolling, Velie," he said. "Drop the suspicion-of-murder charge. I've already talked to the district attorney, and he agrees that without satisfactory answers—and they're not satisfactory—Mrs. McKell is to be formally charged with the murder of Sheila Grey."

Bail was speedily arranged. Ashton McKell had said, "Let's have no nonsense about not accepting bond. One fool in the family is enough."

Lutetia was submissive. Had her husband advised it, she would have marched with equal submissiveness to jail, to make her bed with the prostitutes, drug addicts, shoplifters, and drunks in the euphemistically named House of Detention for Women in Greenwich Village.

Robert O'Brien was *hors de combat*—this *combat*, at any rate. The legal warrior was occupied with another case, also a murder indictment, for the trial of which he had exhausted his last legal delay. "The guy is a professional hood," he told Ashton. "I'm positive he's committed at least two gangland executions with which he's never even been charged, and he'll sure as hell commit more if he gets the opportunity. But he didn't commit this one, and this is the one I'm concerned with. Of course, as soon as we get Falconetti's trial out of the way I'll be back with you, Mr. McKell. But I can't predict just when that will be. You'd better get another lawyer."

The tapestries that had graced the walls of the Château de Saint-Loy—unicorns, vainly coursed by hounds and hunters, captured and gentled by comely virgins; Helen, not yet of Troy, and her retinue departing for Cytherea; King Louis confuting the heathen—looked down upon a scene that was certainly not the least strange they had viewed in their long centuries.

There was Lutetia McKell presiding over her tea service as if nothing had happened. "Wouldn't you like a cup of tea, Judy? You look chilled. I've some of your favorite keemun. Ashton? Dane?"

They exchanged despairing glances. "I don't think any of us wants tea at the moment, Mother," Dane said. "Dad was saying something."

"Forgive me, dear. I'm afraid I wasn't listening closely."

Her husband inhaled. "Lutetia. *Did* you substitute the live cartridges for the blanks?"

"Yes, dear," said Lutetia.

110

Dane cried, *"Why?"*

"Well, darling, you see, when your father lent Miss Grey the revolver, because she was nervous about being alone in the penthouse, he told me about it." Of course. Didn't his father tell her everything? Well, Dane thought grimly, not *everything*. "He'd said he was afraid, however, Miss Grey not being accustomed to firearms and so on, that there might be an accident. So, he told me, he'd put blank bullets in the revolver instead of real ones, although he'd bought live shells at the time he purchased the revolver. That's how I knew, Ashton, that the live cartridges were on the top shelf of your wardrobe."

Ashton groaned.

Lutetia continued in the same bright tone. One day, she said, she had telephoned the penthouse. Sheila Grey's maid, who came in daily, answered. Miss Grey, she had told Lutetia, was out. Lutetia had hung up without giving her name.

She had then dressed properly for a neighborly visit and gone up to the penthouse and rung the bell. The maid answered the door.

"Is Miss Grey in?"

"No, ma'am. I don't expect her for sure till six."

"You mean she *may* return before then? In that case, I believe I'll wait. I'm Mrs. McKell, who lives downstairs."

The maid had hesitated only for a moment. "I guess it'll be all right, ma'am. I recognized you. Come in."

Lutetia had sat down in a chair in Sheila's living room (not a very comfortable one, she said: "I don't care for Swedish Modern, do you, Judy?") and the maid had excused herself. "If you don't mind, ma'am, I've got my work to do."

Although Lutetia had never been in the penthouse apartment during Sheila Grey's occupancy, she was familiar with the apartment's layout. There were only two bedrooms, one a guest room; any woman could tell at a glance which was which, and both lay at the side of the apartment away from the kitchen, which was separated from the living room by a hall. Lutetia waited a few moments, then quietly got up and walked through the door on the other side.

She was wrong about the guest room; there was none.

111

Sheila had converted her second bedroom into a workroom; here was where she plotted her fashions, the GHQ of her organization. With all deliberate speed Lutetia proceeded to the master bedroom.

Logic demanded that the revolver be kept in the night-table drawer. And there it was. She took the weapon, removed its blanks, inserted the live ammunition, returned the revolver to the drawer, and left the bedroom with the blanks clutched in her handkerchief.

She had summoned the maid, said she would not wait after all, and returned to her apartment.

"Then I put the box of bullets in my dressing-table drawer," Lutetia concluded conversationally, "along with the blank ones in the handkerchief. That's all there was to it, darling."

Ashton pounded his palm in frustration. "But why, Lutetia, why?"

"I couldn't think what else to do with them."

"I don't mean that." Her husband passed his hand over his face. "I mean the whole *thing*. Why did you switch cartridges at all? What on earth did you have in mind? Didn't you realize the danger?"

"You don't understand, Ashton. The danger, as you call it, was the whole point. Some night when that woman—girl—would be all alone, I intended to visit her and tell her that I knew all about you and her. I was going to *threaten* her, don't you see?"

"Threaten her?" repeated Ashton, blankly.

"And taunt her, too."

"Mother," rasped Dane, "what are you talking about?"

"And make her so angry that she'd shoot me."

Had Lutetia broken out in Swahili, or Urdu, they could not have regarded her with more bafflement.

"Shoot you," her husband repeated. The words evidently meant nothing to him. "Shoot *you*," he said again.

"*Shoot* you, Mother?"

"Don't you see? It was all my fault, your father's consorting with that woman, turning his back on his wife. If I had been a better, more understanding wife to your father, he would never have taken up with another woman. It was my doing, really. I was the guilty one."

"You're lying!" cried Ashton McKell. "What kind of

112

story is that? Do you expect any grown person to believe such a yarn? Lutetia." He glared at her. "*Did you shoot Sheila?*"

She was staring at him in horror, like a child who, having told the exact turth, is still accused of fibbing. Her lower lip trembled.

"Ashton, *no*. How can you think such a thing? I changed those bullets for the reason I told you. Don't you believe me?"

"No," he flung at her. Then he muttered, "I don't know."

She's insane, Dane thought, with the creeping kind of insanity that just touches the edge of another world, and he doesn't see it. He's still trying to judge her rationally.

The thought was so acute that Dane almost groaned aloud. He had never realized it; now, in the flash of the revelation, it was as if he had known it all his life. Everything was illuminated by it—his mother's unnatural selflessness, her timidities resting on a bedrock of Victorian stubbornness, her self-isolation, her clinging to a past that for her must always be the present. How long has this been coming on? He wondered; and, looking back, it was impossible for him to judge just when she had crossed the line.

Whenever it had been, there was no spark to convert it into action until she became aware of her husband's "spiritual infidelity." Then, in her system of twisted values, she moved; she took the blame on herself by seeking punishment, at the same time that she "protected" her beloved husband and master and laid the onus of punishment on the other woman's shoulders.

What his father must be thinking, Dane could not imagine. The whole concept was so extraordinary—the guilty man shriven of guilt, but feeling guilt still—that probably his thoughts were one boiling confusion. The elder McKell's trapdoor mouth was half open, his commanding eyes glossy, his breathing labored. He looked like a man in shock.

It was Judy Walsh who said gently, "But didn't you realize, Mrs. McKell, that what you did might lead to the accidental death of someone else?" *Judy knew.*

Lutetia shook the head that now rested on the lacy jabot of her bosom. "I'm so sorry. I never thought of that.

How stupid of me. I was so sure it could only happen to me. But it didn't . . . The nights came and went, and they were lonely nights . . . I could never bring myself to carry out my plan."

Judy turned away; her eyes were filled with tears.

"No," Lutetia said slowly. "Somehow, I never went back there."

In Robert O'Brien's unavailability, and on his recommendation, Ashton McKell engaged the services of Henry Calder Barton, a well-known criminal lawyer of the old school. Barton, assisted and advised by Heaton, indicated his line of defense.

"They can certainly show that Mrs. McKell could have done it," Barton said. He was a heavy-set old man with a crop of white hair above a turkey-red face. "But they just as certainly can't prove that she did do it. We'll play the unknown-prowler bit for all it's worth."

"And how much, Mr. Barton," asked Ashton bleakly, "is that?"

"Quite a lot. After all, Sheila Grey was no frightened little old lady seeing burglars under her bed at the shifting of every shadow. As I understand it, she was a shrewd, clearheaded businesswoman, a woman of spirit and action. If a woman like that became suddenly afraid to be alone, it's a reasonable assumption that she had cause, or thought she had. There has been a rash of cases of forcible nocturnal entry in Park Avenue apartments this past year, many of them unsolved, and some very near your building. A prowler might well have got into the penthouse apartment, found a gun while rummaging in the drawers, and used it on being surprised by the occupant. If he was wearing gloves, his prints would not be found. Prints are rarely found on guns, anyway, even when they're handled without gloves on. Yes, I think we can play up the prowler theory very effectively."

Ashton McKell nodded, but his attention seemed elsewhere. Dane doubted that his father was thinking of prowlers, real or imagined, or of Sheila Grey as merely

114

a "shrewd, clearheaded businesswoman." Dane himself knew her as far more than that; what must his father know of her? And now she was dead, and no one's guilt or innocence, no argument or theory, could change the fact for Ashton McKell.

As for Barton, Dane thought he was whistling in the dark. His mother's fingerprints on the blank shells and on two of the lives ones would alone outweigh the heaviest prowler structure Barton could build up in argument.

He took Barton aside. "I think my mother is mentally unstable," he said quietly. "Isn't that a better line of defense?"

The lawyer looked at him sharply. "What makes you think your mother is of unsound mind?"

"That story she tells about why she loaded the gun with live ammunition. That wasn't an act, Mr. Barton, though I know you think it was—I was watching your face . . . I realize now that this has been coming on for a long time."

Barton shook his head. "I don't see how we can effectively use it. It isn't as if she admits having pulled the trigger . . . I think we have a better chance with the prowler line. Let the burden of proof rest on De Angelus. He hasn't got as good a case as he apparently thinks he has. At least in my opinion. There's a long, long step between proving that she loaded the gun and proving that she pulled the trigger, Mr. McKell. Now don't worry. We can always pull in the psychiatrists as a secondary line of defense . . ."

Dane remained unconvinced.

For all the ease with which Dane had accepted her in his arms at the climax of his father's trial, Judy found their relations becoming more distant. She could not read his mind, but there was no mistaking the coldness of his manner. That moment in the courtroom began to appear an unguarded outpost in time, along with their previous embrace in her apartment. Could his mother's predicament account for his increasing withdrawal? Judy wondered painfully. That could not be the only reason, even if it was a reason. Something else was bothering him. But what?

Judy phoned him one night after a strained dinner at the McKells'. Dane had driven her home in almost total silence and left her abruptly.

"Dane, this is Judy."

"Judy?"

She waited. He waited. "Dane, I must know. What's wrong?"

"Wrong?"

"Something is. You seem so . . ."

He laughed. "My father's been tried for murder, my mother is under arrest on the same charge—what could be wrong?"

While Judy angrily blinked back the tears, she heard the connection broken. So she stumbled to bed.

She did not phone him again, and when finally he phoned her she assumed a coldness to match his.

"Yes, Dane."

"I'm just transmitting a message," he said dully. "Dad and I talked to Ellery Queen a while ago, and he wants us to visit him tomorrow. Dad wants you along. Will you come?"

"Of course."

She waited, but he said nothing more, and after a moment she hung up. His voice had never sounded so lifeless. The crazy thought struck her that they were all dead—Dane, his parents, Ellery Queen, herself—and that the only living entity in the universe was Sheila Grey. It made her hate Sheila Grey . . . That was when Judy gave way to her tears.

"Do you own shares in this hospital," Dane asked, "or are they holding you prisoner?"

Ellery was in the same room at the Swedish-Norwegian Hospital; he was in the same chair, his hockey goalie's legs propped up. The casts looked new.

"The legs weren't knitting properly. They've had to monkey around with them." Ellery seemed tired, restless. "It's a good thing I have no serious psychological

116

problems, or I'm sure I'd be thinking of myself as Tou-louse-Lautrec."

"You poor man." Lutetia stooped and kissed him on the brow.

"Thank you, Mrs. McKell," Ellery said. "That hasn't been done to me for a very long time."

Dane was wondering what direction her behavior would take next when she said, "Well, I felt I hadn't thanked you properly for what you did for my husband."

There was a silence. Then Ellery said, "We'll have to do the same for you, won't we? How do matters stand, Mr. McKell?"

There was little to report and, of that little, little that was new. Barton was stilll talking cheerfully.

"I don't doubt an acquittal," Ashton McKell said, convincing on one, perhaps, but his wife. "However, I'd like something better, Mr. Queen, than the equivalent of the Scotch verdict of Not Proven. I don't want any loose ends."

"In this business, Mr. McKell," Ellery said dryly—perhaps he was piqued by a certain commanding-officer quality in the McKell voice—"we generally take what we can get."

He began to talk to Lutetia of inconsequential things —the deadly sameness of hospital life, her taste in flowers (did she like the ones in the vase? would she take one and pin it on her dress?)—nothing, at first, to remind her that today was Friday, and that in three days she would be going on trial for murder.

Gently and step by step (did he suspect? Dane thought) the invalid led Lutetia to describe once more the events of September 14th.

"So after the servants left for the night, you were completely alone, Mrs. McKell?"

"Completely."

"You didn't leave the apartment, even for a few min-utes? For a stroll? Some air?"

No, she had not left the apartment for so much as thirty seconds. Of that she was positive. She had not even gone to the door, because no one had rung or knocked.

117

"How about the telephone? Did you speak to anyone on the phone?"

She hesitated. "Oh, dear."

"Then you did?"

"I think I did."

"To whom?"

"I can't remember. Some man, I think it was."

"About what?"

She smiled uncertainly. "I feel an utter fool. I just don't recall. The only reason I remember a call at all is that I was half expecting my husband to phone from Washington."

"This man called you?"

"Yes."

"You're sure of that."

"I think I'm sure. I'd probably remember if I made a call to anyone."

Dane could have shaken her. "Mother, for heaven's sake, *think*. This could be all-important. Who phoned you?"

"Dane, don't look at me that way. If I remembered, don't you think I'd say? I wasn't paying much attention to anything that evening. You know television. You just sit there in a vacuum . . ."

Yes, Dane thought, where you live most of the time.

". . . and then so much has happened since, it's quite driven the details of that evening out of my head."

"Mrs. McKell, Dane is right," Ellery said. "This could be of the utmost importance. You simply must try to recollect who called you. Was it during the early part of the evening, or late?"

"I don't *know*."

"Was it a wrong number?"

"I don't believe so . . ."

"Someone you knew well?"

"Oh, I'm sure not. A stranger, I'm pretty sure of *that*." This she said brightly, even anxiously, as at a minor triumph that might be snatched away from her. "I suppose that's why I don't remember. It couldn't have been anything of personal importance."

"At the time, perhaps not. Now . . . In any event, you spent the entire evening watching TV—nothing else."

118

"That's correct, Mr. Queen."

"I want you to keep thinking about that call, Mrs. McKell. It will come back to you."

"I'll do my best."

Ellery sagged. He began to rub the bridge of his nose. "We seem to be hung up, don't we? We have your word, Mrs. McKell, that you didn't leave your apartment the entire time. Obviously, if you didn't leave the apartment, you couldn't have shot Miss Grey. The trouble is, we have *only* your word for it. Forgive me if I sound like a bookkeeper . . .

"The problem gets down to the absolute need to substantiate Mrs. McKell's story," Ellery told the others. "How to do that is the heart of the business. Her only contact with the outside world, unless she can remember who phoned her, was by way of the television set. Too bad we don't live in an era of two-way TV communication, as in the science-fiction stories. Well! We seem to have arrived exactly nowhere."

He sounded fagged; his whole personality appeared to have changed since their discussions of Ashton McKell's predicament.

"Let me keep thinking about this," he said. "I'll discuss it with my father, too."

"But he's in charge of the police end of the case," Dane protested.

"Exactly."

It was an unsatisfactory session all around. They rose to go in an atmosphere of helpless gloom. The very air in the room smelled stale.

They were at the door when Ellery suddenly said, "Oh, one thing. It probably won't lead anywhere—"

"Just tell me what it is, Mr. Queen," said Ashton McKell.

"I'm curious about Sheila Grey's work. I'd like to see her fashion designs. What's her establishment called?"

"The House of Grey."

Ellery nodded. "Can you bring me her drawings, photos, advertisements—anything you can lay your hands on of her creative work, or get permission to borrow? Particularly recent material. But I would like to get an all-over picture, going years back, if necessary."

"Why, Mr. Queen?"

119

"If I could answer that, I wouldn't need the material. Say it's a hunch."

"I don't know if we can . . ."

"I'll get it," Dane said. "I'll go to work on it right away. Is that all, Mr. Queen?"

"No, when you do bring me the material I'd appreciate Miss Walsh's coming along with you. You can describe the annual collections to me from a woman's point of view, Miss Walsh—I'm afraid I know as little as most men about women's fashions. Will you do that?"

They left him pulling at his lip, and squinting along the bulky line of his casts.

Sheila Grey had died intestate. Her estate fell to an only relative living in Kansas, a sister with a well-to-do invalid husband. Mrs. Potter had no need for money and no interest in The House of Grey. She had asked the staff to carry on for the time being, had signed powers of attorney, had given John Leslie $100 and the request that he "look after things" in the penthouse apartment; and immediately after the funeral she had flown back home.

Dane told Leslie what it was they wanted.

"I don't know, Mr. Dane," the doorman said. "Seems like it wouldn't be right, me letting anybody take anything from Miss Grey's apartment. Even you, sir. I could get into trouble."

"Suppose it was okay with the police," Dane said. "Would you do it then, John?"

"Sure, sir."

Dane called Ellery; Ellery called his father; Inspector Queen called Sergeant Velie. In the end, Dane got what Ellery wanted. As the Inspector said, "If he can borrow a defendant, I don't see any harm in letting him have a look at some drawings."

Sheila Grey had been systematic in her filing. With Sergeant Velie standing by, Dane and Judy went through the dead woman's workroom in the penthouse. From 1957 on, everything was neatly in place, in chronological order. Under the sergeant's eye they transferred the contents of the files into boxes they had brought for

120

the purpose. Dane signed a receipt, the sergeant counter-signed it, John Leslie went off happy, and at 10 A.M. Saturday, Dane and Judy presented themselves, *cum* boxes, in the Queen room at the Swedish-Norwegian Hospital.

Ellery perked up at sight of them. A quick riffle through some of the material, and he gestured toward the walls. "I had my Valkyrie nurse buy up all the local stocks of Scotch tape. Let's start to the right of the door and tape everything up in the proper time se-quence . . . all around the room—drawings, photos, ads, what-have-you. And if the walls give out, spread them on the floor. You'll note that I persuaded the med-ical powers to let me abandon my chair for a wheel-chair. That's for mobility.

"Judy, you arrange. Dane, you tape. I'll ask questions if and as the spirit—and my ignorance—move."

Judy set to work. She handed Dane the material per-taining to Sheila Grey's first-shown collection, late in 1957, and he taped them to the wall. In a short time Judy was moved to voice her pleasure.

"Aren't these Lady Sheila things stunning," she ex-claimed. "Even if they are six years out of date."

"Lady Sheila?" Ellery said.

"That's the name of that particular collection." Judy pointed. "Each showing has a special collection-name, you see. The next year, 1958, is called Lady Nella. To name a collection gives it more character than just a date. Here—1959—"

"Lady Ruth," Ellery read. "Mmm. Sheila was her own name, so that was natural enough. Nella sounds a bit fancy, but I suppose the exotic touch is an asset in this mysterious business. But why Ruth? Kind of Plain Jane, isn't it? Although . . . yes, I see."

Dane, who did not, said, "See what, Mr. Queen?"

"Ruth. Named after the matron of the same name in the Bible book of ditto, I'll bet a ruffle. I don't know what an archeologist would say, but you could put these dresses—some of them, anyway—on 1000-Girls-1000 in any self-respecting Hollywood Biblical extravaganza and I, for one, wouldn't detect a false note. That beauti-fully ancient simplicity of drape and design. Right, Judy?"

Judy said, "Oh, yes!" Her eyes were shining at the drawings of Sheila Grey's 1960 collection, named Lady Lorna D., with its subtle influences of Scotch color and pattern—gowns which were not so much kilts as kilty, hats which instantly evoked the tam-o'-shanter and Highland bonnet without being either, purses worn in the manner of sporrans but made from the same material as the gown, hinting of plaids and tartans.

"Lady Lorna D.," Ellery mused. "D. for Doone, I suppose. *Was* that Scottish? Well, it doesn't matter. What's next, Judy?"

Next—as the drawings and photographs, the slick pages from *Vogue* and *Harper's Bazaar,* marched around the walls—came Lady Dulcea, 1961. Lady Dulcea educed nothing of the past or of far-off exotica; that collection had aimed at the future, and some of its designs might have gone well with a space helmet. Judy shook her head. "I don't care much for these, compared with the others, I mean. I'm sure it wasn't her most popular collection. Of course, Sheila Grey never had a style showing that could really be called a failure."

"Why Dulcea, I wonder?" asked Ellery. "Any notion, Judy?"

Judy looked dubious. She was already absorbed in the 1962 collection, Lady Thelma, with its daring lines, bold colors, and generally theatrical air. "Isn't it gorgeous? No wonder it was such a sensation."

Dane had used up all the available wall space, and the final group was accordingly spread out on the floor.

"What's this?" Ellery muttered. "This" was the collection Sheila Grey had been working on at the time of her death. In this one there were no photographs, no newspaper articles, no slick magazine illustrations, only drawings. Drawings in various stages of completion, from rough sketches through elaborate mock-ups to the almost-fully-delineated.

"Doesn't look as if she actually got to finish any of them—even these," Ellery said. He was squinting hard.

Judy picked up a drawing. "This one looks finished," she said, handing it to him. "The only one in the batch." At the bottom of the drawing was what was obviously intended to represent the 1963 collection's name.

In inked block capitals: LADY NORMA.

"Well, that's it," said Judy.

Ellery sat bent over in his wheelchair. He nodded slowly. "I wonder if her death could in any way be connected with the intense rivalries that exist in the world of fashion design. It's hardly credible that any reputable salon would send a thug or a thief to break into the Grey apartment. But suppose some independent operator—a free-lance industrial spy—decided to snatch what he could and sell it somewhere . . ."

Dane remembered what Sheila had told him on the subject. Ellery listened closely, interrupting: "Did she name names?" "Did she seem seriously worried?" Then he dropped that line of inquiry and turned to Judy. But Judy could contribute nothing that had any relevance to the murder. Finally he wheeled his chair around the room, examining the material on the walls with the most concentrated care.

He was still in silent communion with Sheila Grey's handiwork when the blond nurse came in with a doctor.

"I'm afraid you two will have to excuse me now."

"Shall we come back this afternoon?" Dane asked Ellery.

"No, you'd better give me some time to digest all this."

In the corridor, Dane and Judy exchanged despairing glances. It would not have cheered them to know that in his hospital room Ellery wore very much the same look.

Judy and Dane met on Sunday. Neither found much to say. Finally Judy could stand it no longer.

"Do you feel as discouraged as I do?"

"I'll match my dragging chin against yours any day."

"You know, we're a couple of goops," Judy said. "I don't see that we're accomplishing anything moping and comparing moods. Why don't we have another look at Sheila Grey's apartment? Maybe we overlooked something."

"For two reasons: One, we have no right to enter the premises; two, the police have been over it half a dozen times, and we're not very likely to find something they missed." They were seated stiffly in the drawing room of the McKell apartment. Ashton and Lutetia had gone to an afternoon church service. "Anyway, nobody overlooked anything."

"Why can't we try? What harm will it do?"

"I told you. We have no right to enter the premises!"

"Dane McKell, don't you raise your voice to me. I'm only trying to help."

"Then suggest something helpful!"

Judy blew up. "Why are you treating me so brutally?"

"I'm not treating you any way at all!"

"There could be something in *that*. Look, buster, I know what's eating you. You can't forgive yourself because one night, for a few seconds, you allowed yourself to forget that little Miss Secretary, your father's hired hand, came from the wrong side of the elevated tracks!"

"Oh, come on, Judy," Dane said wearily.

"Also, I have the misfortune to be Irish. And not lace-curtain Irish, either!"

"I wouldn't care if you were a Hottentot."

"You'd treat me just as badly, is that it?"

"Now you're talking like a female. It's nothing you *are*, Judy. The trouble is me."

"Don't give me that baloney," Judy said tautly. "We worked together so well for a while, until I forgot my place. You haven't spoken a decent word to me since."

"Judy, try to understand." A certain faltering, the way his features twisted, silenced Judy. "It's something about me. Personally. I can't explain it. I mean, I may never be able to. Even to you. Especially to you."

"I *don't* understand."

"Look, maybe John Leslie can be wheedled into letting us into the penthouse after all. Let's give your suggestion a workout."

It was merely a way of terminating their conversation. Leslie, who with the passage of time seemed to have a deepening respect for the law, could not be wheedled, even by Dane; they argued with him half-heartedly, and with each other snappishly; and finally Judy left Dane in a huff, refusing his offer to see her home.

The next day, Monday, when the trial began, Dane and Judy Walsh were seated on opposite sides of the courtroom aisle.

124

The trial of Lutetia McKell was not quite a duplicate of her husband's. For one thing, the selection of a jury took almost no time at all. For another, the proceedings developed in an altogether different atmosphere, a here-we-go-again climate that produced more curiosity than heat. The feeling was generated that the district attorney was about to make an ass of himself. As one newspaper put it, "If at first you don't succeed, prosecute the wife." It was not fair to De Angelus, but newspaperdom is rarely concerned with fairness.

Henry Barton seized the opportunity. Ridicule became his not-so-secret weapon in cross-examination of prosecution witnesses, and what he could not attack with ridicule he undermined by innuendo. For example, when Detective Mack was on the stand to recount his and Sergeant Velie's various visits to the McKell apartment, the attorney for the defense said, "Now Detective Mack, you've been assigned to this precinct for—how long is it?"

"Two years."

"Let's take the past six months. Have you had occasion to visit other apartments in other apartment buildings in the neighborhood of the McKell building in the past six months?"

"Yes, sir."

"On official busniess?"

"Yes, sir."

"In your capacity as a police detective?"

"Yes, sir."

"To investigate cases of forcible entry, armed robbery, burglary, and so forth?"

"Yes, sir."

"One case only last August *in the very next building to the McKells'?*"

"Yes, sir, but—"

"In that case a housemaid was tied up and the lady of the house assaulted and robbed?"

The district attorney objected strenuously on the usual ground of improper cross, and a pretty by-play de-

125

veloped among the lawyers and the judge, the result of which was that the questions and answers along this line were ordered stricken; but the impression was implanted in the jury's mind that the neighborhood of the McKell apartment building was a regular prey of prowlers, which was what Barton was trying to establish.

On the morning of the third day of the trial, Ellery was glumly studying a color photograph of a gaunt model in an evening gown from Sheila Grey's Lady Dulcea collection when he was rather violently visited by the McKells, father and son.

He sat up alertly, shifting his casts to a less uncomfortable position. "Something up?"

"Last week when you were questioning my wife," Ashton McKell said, eyes glittering, "do you remember your saying that the television set was her only contact with the outside world?"

"Yes?"

"Look at this!"

"It came," Dane said, "in this morning's mail."

It was an envelope addressed to "Mrs. Ashton Mc-Kell" at the Park Avenue address. The enclosure, on the stationery of The Princess Soap Company, was signed by a Justin A. Lattimoore, Fourth Vice-President.

Ellery smiled as he read it:

My dear Mrs. McKell:

Our Accounting Department advises me that our check in the amount of five hundred dollars ($500.00), which was posted to you more than three months ago as your prize in the Lucky Number segment of our Princess Hour TV program on the night of September 14th last, has never been cashed.

I am accordingly writing to inquire if you have received the above check. If not, or if for some reason you do not wish to cash it, will you please communicate with us at your early convenience?

Yours very truly, *etc.*

"Well," Ellery said. "This could be the straw that breaks the district attorney's back."

"It is," said Dane. "It has to be!"

"Now let's not get our hopes up too high," his father

126

cautioned excitedly. "What I can't understand is why Lutetia didn't *tell* us."

"Don't you know Mother, Dad? She just forgot, that's all!"

"But a prize?" murmured Ellery. "A check?"

"What is money to her, or she to money?" Dane misquoted happily. "And prizes mean publicity. Her mind recoils reflexively from such things. This could be the break, Mr. Queen. It really could."

"We'll see. Get in touch with this Lattimoore fellow and see if you can't get him up here. We've got to find out all we can about this, and right away."

One telephone call from the eminent Ashton McKell insured the presence of Fourth Vice-President Justin A. Lattimoore in the Queen hospital room that afternoon. Lattimoore proved to be a fastidiously groomed gentleman with a face the precise shade of flesh-colored grease paint, and (Ellery was positive) with a toupee. He could not seem to decide whether to be more honored by the summons of a captain of industry than supercilious at the sight of a mere writer with two legs in a cast; in any event, he contrived to convey the impression that he was in the company of at least one peer.

" . . . a quarter-hour morning program for Sudsy Chippos," Mr. Lattimoore was saying, evidently feeling that the occasion called for a recapitulation of The Princess Soap Company's radio and television schedule, "and another quarter-hour in mid-afternoon for our Princess Belinda and Princess Anita toiletries. In other words, the A.M. show is *Doctor Dolly's Family,* and the P.M. show is *Life and Laurie Lewis.*

"For TV last season The Princess Hour was a variety show emceed by Bo Bunson, the comedian. I will be frank, gentlemen," Vice-President Lattimoore said handsomely. "The variety show was a bomb, or suds down the drain, as we say at the shop. Rating-wise, it reeked.

"For this season one of our ad agency's brighter young men came up with a real doozer. We could not scrap the variety show"—Lattimoore coughed—"our Chairman of the Board has great faith in it, and thinks Bunson is the funniest man in show business—but we would add a gimmick to the format. Throughout the show—we're on Wednesday nights in prime time, ten to eleven P.M. in the East, as you undoubtedly know—throughout the show a battery of telephone operators would call up people picked out of phone books all over the country by a process I won't bother to describe, and ask them if they were watching the Princess Hour.

"Of course, most of them said yes, and immediately turned to our channel if they weren't watching already. The yes answerers were switched onto the air between numbers, Bo Bunson talked to them over the phone personally—on the air—and each one was given the chance to guess the Lucky Number for that night's show. The Lucky Number, which could be any number between 1 and 10,000, was selected at random by an IBM machine before we went on the air, and no one, not even the emcee, knew what it was—he had it in a sealed envelope and at strategic spots during the show he exhibited the envelope and made wisecracks about it—supposed to be stimulating suspense-wise, you see."

Ellery mumbled that he did indeed see; his tone suggested that, for purposes of the subject under discussion, he wished he were temporarily sightless. For the fraction of a moment uncertainty flickered over Mr. Lattimoore's baby face, which looked as if he scrubbed every hour on the hour with Princess Belinda and Princess Anita soaps, and perhaps with Sudsy Chippos as well—but then the smile flashed back on with no kilowatt impaired.

"The gimmick was that everybody won. First prize was $10,000—that was for anyone who guessed a number within 25 of the actual Lucky Number. Say the Lucky Number turned out to be 8,951. Any number picked by a contestant between 8,926 and 8,976 would be considered a bull's-eye; if more than one contestant scored a bull's-eye, the number closest to the Lucky Number was considered first-prize winner, the next closest getting second prize, which was $2,000. Third money went to the next closest, $1,000; fourth prize to the next closest, $500; all others got $100 consolation prizes.

"Quite an idea, wasn't it?" glowed Mr. Lattimoore; but then the glow dimmed. "The only trouble was, it lasted a mere four weeks. Not only did B. T. consider it a flop with knobs on because, he said, it lowered the dignity of Princess products—that's B. T. Worliss, Chairman of the Board—but there were, frankly, hrrm, legal problems, very serious ones. Having to do with the anti-lottery laws. The FCC . . ." Mr. Lattimoore stopped, the dread initials sticking in this throat. He cleared it. "Well, that's the story of the ill-fated numbers game," he said with feeble levity. "What else can I tell you gentlemen?"

"And on the telecast of September 14th," Ellery mumbled, shading his eyes from the Lattimoore effulgence, "Mrs. McKell was one of the lucky persons telephoned?"

"That's right. She came out fourth in our little old guessing game. Took the $500 prize."

"And the check was never cashed."

Ashton McKell produced a pink check. "And here it is, Mr. Queen. Lutetia simply isn't used to handling money. She meant to send it to the Church Home, the one she does her needlework for, but she clean forgot."

When Henry Calder Barton rose to open the defense, he wore a look in marked contrast to the expression of lofty confidence he had displayed previously. The actor was stripped away. Henry Barton had a good thing going suddenly, and he could afford to dispense with the psychology.

He went to work briskly.

"Mr. Graves, you are an assistant account executive with Newby, Fellis, Herkimer, Hinsdale and Levy, an advertising agency located on Madison Avenue? Your firm handles the Princess Soap account for television and radio?"

"Yes."

Barton led the man skillfully through a description of how the defunct numbers game, a recent feature of The Princess Soap Company's TV evening hour, worked.

"Thank you, Mr. Graves."

De Angelus did not cross-examine; he objected. The consultation with Judge Everett Hershkowitz before the bench evidently satisfied His Honor, for he overruled the objection and the district attorney sat down to torment a fingernail. Barton's new look had not escaped him.

"Call Miss Hattie Johnson."

"Miss Johson, what is your line of work?"

"I am a special telephone operator."

"You do not work for the telephone company itself?"

"No, sir, for Tel-Operator, Incorporated." Tel-Operator, Incorporated, turned out to be a firm that supplied operators for private corporations which required a type of answering service that the regular answering services were not prepared to furnish. Usually, the witness explained, this special service was for a limited period of time, such as after a "premium offer" was advertised for sale by a department store, and so on. "We have to be very quick and accurate," Miss Johnson said.

"And were you one of the operators assigned to The Princess Soap Company's television show Lucky Number gimmick?"

"Yes, sir, on Wednesday nights, for the four weeks it lasted."

"Do you recall your work in connection with the telecast of Wednesday, September 14th last, Miss Johnson?"

"I do. That was the first show we worked."

"I show you this transcript. Do you recognize it?"

"Yes, sir. It is a copy of one of my telephone conversations with a person I called that night."

"Who was the person? Read the name from the transcript, Miss Johnson."

" 'Mrs. Ashton McKell, 610½ Park Avenue, New York City.' "

Judge Hershkowitz had to resort to his gavel. District Attorney De Angelus was observed to inhale deeply, as after a long run, then fold his arms defensively across his chest.

Barton placed the transcript in evidence. Its contents, read aloud by the witness, almost broke up the court, and the Court almost broke up his gavel. As for the district attorney, he was blitzed.

When order was restored, Barton called Lutetia McKell to the stand.

130

"—but how could you have forgotten the call, Mrs. McKell? When so much depended on it?"

"I don't know," Lutetia replied helplessly. "I did remember speaking to some man over the phone—"

"Was that Bo Bunson, Master of Ceremonies of the Princess Soap show?"

"Yes, I remember him now. But I'm afraid none of the conversation struck me with any sense of importance. It all seemed so silly, in fact, my mind simply dropped it out of sight."

"In any event, you remember the call now?"

"Yes."

"You remember winning $500 as a result of that call?"

"Now I do."

"You're a very wealthy woman, Mrs. McKell?"

"I beg your pardon? Surely—"

"And all your financial affairs are handled by others? Your husband? Your family attorney? Banks, and so forth?"

"Oh, yes."

"Then you're not accustomed to handling money?"

"I'm afraid not."

The D.A. was watching her with admiration, almost affection. The same expression in varying degrees touched the faces of the judge, Barton himself, and Inspector Queen, who was sitting in on the trial and had testified for the prosecution.

"Tell us about your telephone conversation that night with Mr. Bunson."

"I'm afraid I didn't understand the game very well. I do not watch television as a rule, and it's been very long since I played games. When—Mr. Bunson, is it?—asked me to guess the Lucky Number, I simply could not think of a number. Any at all. It was so peculiar. My mind just froze. Has that ever happened to you?" She was half turned in the witness chair between Henry Barton and Judge Hershkowitz, and it was a tribute to her palpable helplessness that both men responded to it with sympathetic nods. "At any rate, not wishing to disappoint the young man on the TV, and happening at that moment to notice the studio clock above his head, I think I said something like, 'Does it matter where I get the number?'

131

and he said something that must have been comical, because the studio audience laughed—I don't recall just what it was—and then I said, 'Oh, dear, the only number I can think of is the time the clock over your head shows—twenty-two minutes past ten. So I'll say 1022.'"

"1022," Henry C. Barton said to the jury in his summation. "Hold on to that number, ladies and gentlemen, because it's going to direct you to clear my client of the charge for which she's being tried.

"Ten. Twenty. Two.

"At twenty-two minutes past the hour of ten o'clock on the night Sheila Grey was shot to death, Lutetia McKell in her own voice and person was answering the telephone in the McKell apartment. You have examined the photostatic evidence of the telephone operator's handwritten report—Mrs. McKell's name, her address, her telephone number, the exact time the operator called her and she answered in the McKell apartment. You have listened to an excerpt from the taped recording of the actual show as it was telecast, and you have heard the unmistakable voice of Mrs. McKell talking to Mr. Bunson while the show was on the air, and you have heard her point out the time on the studio clock and use it as her number entry in the guessing game.

"1022.

"There was no collusion. This was by no stretch of anyone's imagination a put-up job. The advertising agency did not invent this game, The Princess Soap Company did not pay for its production and telecast, all to provide an alibi for Lutetia McKell. Nor is there any way in the world that Lutetia McKell could have anticipated that she would be called at the exact time to provide her with an alibi. These are hard facts, and hard facts do not lie.

"At 10:22 P.M. Lutetia McKell was *in* her own apartment, speaking over the phone in the hearing of millions of TV viewers.

"At 10:23 P.M. Miss Grey was shot and killed in *her* apartment two stories above the McKells'.

132

"One minute later. Sixty seconds!"

Barton took a little stroll before the jury to allow his words time to sink into their heads.

"Ladies and gentlemen of the jury, I do not envy the prosecution its job. The district attorney—for all the evidence he has presented about cartridges, revolvers, and fingerprints; for all his charges of jealousy—has the impossible task of asking this jury of intelligent men and women to believe that Mrs. McKell—who, while certainly not showing her years, still is no longer at the Olympic Games sprinter age—hung up her telephone after talking to Bo Bunson, left her apartment, rang and waited for the elevator or sprinted up two flights of stairs (can you see Mrs. McKell sprinting, ladies and gentlemen?) to the penthouse, surreptitiously and cautiously gained entry to the Grey apartment—and I would have you remember that at no time have the People introduced evidence to indicate that Mrs. McKell had any means of gaining that entry to the Grey apartment—surreptitiously and cautiously stole into Miss Grey's bedroooom, searched for the revolver, found the revolver, sneaked into Miss Grey's workroom, confronted Miss Grey long enough for the poor woman to cry out, and then shot her to death . . . *all in sixty seconds!*

"I defy Jesse Owens in his prime to do it! I invite the district attorney to try it himself. It simply couldn't be done. It was a physical and temporal impossibility.

"Ladies and gentlemen, there is only one point for you to consider in judging the guilt or innocence of this defendant: Did Lutetia McKell, at precisely 10:23 P.M. on the night of September 14th, shoot Sheila Grey to death in the Grey apartment, or did she not? She did not. She did not, and you now know she did not. And the reason you know she did not is simply that she could not. *She had not time.*"

The case went to the jury at a quarter past eleven on December 23rd, after a brief charge by Judge Hershkowitz ("You are to consider only the question: Did the defendant on the night of September 14th, at 10:23 P.M., fire the shot that killed Sheila Grey? If the defendant did, she is guilty of murder as charged in the indictment. If you find that she did not fire the shot, then you

133

must find that she is not guilty of the crime as charged in the indictment. In making your decision, you must consider the testimony you have heard in this courtroom concerning the accused's telephone conversation at about that same time. If you hold that testimony to be relevant, you must then consider the matter of timing. This court believes the matter of timing in this case to be all-important . . ."). At half-past noon the jury had reached a verdict, when the defense attorney and the district attorney had not yet returned from their lunch (the judge, an old hand, had lunch sent into his chambers). Barton and De Angelus, notified, scurried back to the courtroom with their lunches half consumed.

The headline on the tabloid that was first to print the news, FREE LU, was not—as some English-speaking foreigner might have interpreted—an imperative; it was a statement of what the jury had in fact done.

Dane's mother was acquitted, as her husband before her had been.

Judge Hershkowitz said to the jury, "Your verdict is justified by the evidence . . . Two indictments have now been returned for the murder of Sheila Grey, and in each case the jury, having seen and heard the evidence, has refused to convict. The killer is, accordingly, still at large. We do not wish an innocent person to be pronounced guilty; at the same time we do not wish a guilty person to escape unpunished."

This last was taken—accurately—by police, district attorney's office, and press alike as a juridical nudge to get on with the job, and this time do it right.

The McKells were too overjoyed to weigh nuances. Ashton exclaimed, "What a wonderful Christmas present. We'll all be together on the Twenty-fifth, and without this nightmare hanging over us. Mr. Barton, how can I express my gratitude?"

The lawyer shook his head. "Don't thank me, thank that fellow Lattimoore and his uncashed $500 check. All I did was follow through. With that evidence, any kid fresh out of law school could have earned an acquittal."

The only one present who was not happily jabbering away was Lutetia herself. When Dane asked her why

134

she was so preoccupied, his mother said, "It will always be on my conscience."

"What, Mother?"

"Replacing the blank cartridges in that revolver with live ones. Why did I do it? She would still be alive—"

"Stop it, Mother. This instant."

It took them a long time to restore her spirits. At one point Dane got the impression that she would have been content to give herself up and stand trial all over again. As he said to his father, "Thank God for the rule of double jeopardy!"

Henry Calder Barton did not leave the courtroom with them. He went over to talk to the district attorney, who was talking to Inspector Queen.

"As His Honor would say, Henry, *mazel tov,*" De Angelus said sourly.

"What are you congratulating him for?" snarled old man Queen. "A baby could have walked off with this case. Soap!"

Barton grinned. "I couldn't agree more, Inspector. Uh . . . Mr. D.A. I know this isn't the best time in the world to ask if you'll let my client, that Gogarty boy, cop a plea for manslaughter. But it would save everybody time and money. What do you say?"

De Angelus grunted, "It sure as hell isn't. Do you realize that lightning has struck me twice in this Grey murder? With Dick Queen here standing under the same tree?"

"Why take it out on Gogarty?"

"Talk to me about it tomorrow. Today I wouldn't make bargains with my own mother."

"Why, Teddy, you wouldn't be disgruntled because two innocent people have been found not guilty, would you?"

"Look, Henry, I'm unhappy, Inspector Queen's unhappy, everybody's unhappy except you and the McKells. So let's leave it at Merry Christmas, huh?"

Ellery was unhappy, too, the impending Christmas never having seemed less Merry. For one thing, he would have to spend it in the hospital; and the half-promise of his doctor that he might be home and hobbling around before the New Year carried exactly as much conviction as half-promises usually do.

He was now mobile to the extent of wheeling himself about the corridors, so he helped the ravishing blond nurse decorate the Christmas tree on their floor, and he almost enjoyed the Swedish *julotta* celebration afterward. But the only real pleasure he took was in the joy of the McKell family.

His unhappiness had a broader base, a disdainful disappointment in himself. Armchair detective! What satisfaction he had taken in his role in the case of Ashton McKell—Phase One, as he had come to think of it—was erased by his nonexistent role in Phase Two. By himself he had come up with nothing whatever to help Lutetia. That letter from The Princess Soap Company, from which her subsequent acquittal stemmed, had simply turned up one morning through the courtesy of the ineffable Lattimoore. Its import would have been obvious to a rookie policeman.

And the killer of Sheila Grey was still at large, as Judge Hershkowitz had pointed out, and the great man hadn't a clue in his head that might be called promising.

Oh, well, Ellery thought with a sigh. At least the McKells' troubles are over.

The McKells' troubles were over for exactly one weekend. Father, mother, and son had had a pleasant, if not joyous, Christmas together. They had attended services at the great unfinished cathedral on Christmas Eve, mingling unnoticed with the crowds of worshipers. In the morning they attended services at a chapel in a poor neighborhood whose congregation was almost entirely foreign-born and whose "language" newspaper had run no photograph of the McKell family. The remainder of Christmas Day they spent quietly at home. They had exchanged gifts, listened to the *Missa Solemnis* on the hifi, read the newspapers.

On Monday, Lutetia expressed a desire to see the ocean. Ramon had been given the day off, for Ashton was at home—the McKell enterprises, like most companies, were keeping Monday as part of the holiday—so Dane drove his parents down to Long Beach, where for almost two hours they strolled beside the gray Atlantic sweeping endlessly in from Europe. The walk made them hungry, and when they returned home Lutetia took pleasure in preparing a hearty supper of soup and sirloin steak with her own hands. Ashton read aloud from Matthew, they listened to the enchanting music of Buxtehude's *Missa Brevis* and the majestic Mendelssohn *Elijah* sung ineffably by the Huddersfield Choral Society, and then they called it a day.

Dane was still eating breakfast as well as dining with his parents; he supposed this would stop when he could slip his life back into its independent groove once more, an opportunity he was on the lookout for these days. He was at breakfast in his parents' apartment, then, two days after Christmas, when Ramon—waiting to drive Ashton to his office—brought in the mail containing the bulky brown envelope.

Ashton, shuffling through the mail, handed the brown envelope to Dane. It was a long one made of kraft paper. Dane slit it open, removed its contents, glanced over them—and the cup he set down in the saucer rattled.

"Dane?" said Lutetia. "Is something the matter?"

He continued to read; his complexion had turned gluey.

"Son, what is it?" Ashton asked.

Dane muttered, "Now it will have to come out."

"What will have to come out?"

Dane rose. "I'll tell you, Dad. But first I've got to make a phone call."

Automatically he went to his old room, sat down at his old desk. For a moment he buried his face in his hands. Then he got a grip on himself and dialed a number.

"Judy?"

"Dane." She sounded remote.

"Judy, I can tell you now what I wasn't able to tell you before." The words came tumbling out. "About what's been worrying me—making me act toward you the way I . . . Please. Would you—can you—meet me right away in Ellery Queen's room at the hospital?"

Judy said uncertainly, "All right." She hung up.

"Dane," Ashton McKell said from the doorway; Lutetia was peering anxiously from behind him. "You said you'd tell me."

"Come with me to see Ellery Queen, Dad. Mother, not you."

"Your mother will stay here."

"Whatever you think best, dear."

Left alone, Lutetia frowned out her picture window. The world outside was hurrying so. Trouble, always trouble. Ever since . . . But Lutetia shut her mind down very firmly. That way lay unpleasantness. There was always one's duty, no matter how trifling, for relief. She rang for her maid. "Margaret, I shall want my needlework. Tell Helen she may begin clearing off the breakfast things."

Ellery greeted them with ebullience. "It's official," he chortled. "I'll be out of this Bastille in a few days." Then he said, in a different tone, "What's up now?"

Dane handed him the kraft envelope. He peered in. Inside lay a smaller envelope, which he took out; pasted to the smaller envelope was a photograph of three written words: *For the Police.* Inside the smaller envelope, as in a Chinese puzzle box, there was an envelope smaller still, and on it was pasted a photo of a complete handwritten sentence: *To be opened only in the event I die of unnatural causes.* And inside the innermost envelope he found the photograph of a holograph statement about three-quarters of an ordinary page long.

Ellery's head shot up.

"Sheila Grey," he said sharply. "Is this her handwriting?"

Dane nodded bitterly. Ashton said, "I've examined it, compared it with, well, some letters I have. It's her handwriting without a doubt." There was nothing in his expression at all, nothing. Only his voice betrayed him.

Ellery glanced over the letter. Every jot of the photographed handscript stood out starkly.

"Miss Walsh." He held the photo out to her. "Read this aloud. I want to hear it in a woman's voice."

"Mr. Queen."

"Please."

Judy took it from him as if it were smeared with filth. She began to read; twice she had to pause to swallow.

" 'Dane McKell tonight asked if he could come up to my apartment for a nightcap,' " Judy read. " 'I told him I had work to do, but he insisted. In the apartment he refused to leave and nothing I could say made him do so. I lost my temper and slapped him. He then tried to . . .' "

Here Judy's voice faltered altogether. Ellery said harshly, "Go on, please."

" 'He then tried to strangle me,' " Judy whispered. " 'This is not hysteria on my part—he actually tried to strangle me. He took my throat . . . in his hands and . . . squeezed and seemed to be out of his mind with an . . . with an insane rage.' I can't, Mr. Queen, I just *can't* go on!"

Ellery read the rest of it himself, rapidly. " 'As he choked me he screamed that he was going to kill me and he called me many obscene names. Then he dropped me to the floor and ran out of the apartment. In another minute I would have been dead of strangulation. I am convinced that he is a dangerous person and I repeat his name, Dane McKell. He definitely tried to kill me. Signed, Sheila Grey.' "

"And I thought the McKell tribe was out of the woods," Dane said hollowly. He laughed.

No one laughed with him. Judy was blinking back tears as she stared out the hospital window; Ashton was frowning at Ellery, but not as if he could see him. Ellery set the letter down.

"First," he said. "Assuming Sheila Grey to have written the original of this letter—Dane, is what she wrote true?"

139

Dane stared at his hands. "When I was a kid at school there was a boy named Philbrick, a stupid kid, I don't even recall any more what he looked like, only that his nose was always running. He said to me, 'If your father's name is Ashton, yours ought to be Ashcan.' Just silly kid talk, nonsense. But he kept at it. 'Ashcan.' Every time he saw me, 'Ashcan.' He knew I hated it. One night we were getting ready to go to bed. As he'd said a hundred times before, he jeered, 'Ashcan, you left your towel in the shower.' I went wild. Jumped him, knocked him down, got my hands around his throat, began to throttle him. I'd certainly have succeeded if some of the other boys hadn't pulled me off. You remember, Dad. I was almost kicked out.

"Yes, it's all true, Mr. Queen, what Sheila wrote," Dane muttered. "If sanity hadn't returned in time . . ."

"Dane's always had a terrible temper, Mr. Queen," Ashton said. "We had considerable trouble about that when he was a boy." He stopped as if to digest the past, made a little gesture of bewilderment. "I thought that was all over, son."

"So did I, God damn it! Well, it isn't."

"I surely thought you'd conquered it. I surely thought so."

Ellery was staring at the photographic paper. "I wonder just when that night she wrote this."

"It must have been after I left," Ashton said. "You remember I got there just a shade before ten o'clock, and there was no indiciation that she'd been writing. She was crying."

"So she wrote it in the fifteen minutes or so between your leaving," Ellery mused, "and her killer's arrival." He was poking about in the small envelope. "What's this?"

"Read it," growled Dane, "and weep."

Ellery took from it a note written in anonymous block capital lettering, with an ordinary pencil, on a ragged-edged sheet apparently torn out of a cheap memorandum book.

The note read:

MR. DANE MCKELL. SHEILA GREY'S LETTER WON'T BE SENT TO POLICE *IF*. MAKE

UP PLAIN PACKAGE 100 $20 BILLS NOT
MARKED AND MAIL TO MR. I.M. ECKS CARE
GENERAL DELIVERY MAIN POST OFFICE
CITY. IMMEDIATE. THEN PACK OF $1000 IN
$20 BILLS, NOT MARKED, TO BE SENT 15TH
OF EVERY MONTH WITHOUT FAIL SAME
ADDRESS. OR POLICE WILL BE INFORMED. I
MEAN THIS.

"Mr. I. M. Ecks. A comedian," Ellery commented. "I
must say I don't blame you for not finding him funny."

"Blackmail." Dane let out the same bitter laugh.
"What do I do?"

"What I did," his father said quietly.

"What?" Dane said.

"You paid someone blackmail, too, Mr. McKell?" Ellery turned quickly back from the etched trees he had
been studying through his window.

"I got a similar letter—I'm sure the same person sent
it, from the kind of note it is, the wording, the paper and
so on—shortly after, well, I began visiting Miss Grey."
Ashton McKell swallowed. "It was foolish of me, I
know. But I just couldn't face a scandal. So I paid—
$2,000 down, $1,000 a month. It was worth that to me
to keep my name and family from being dragged
through the newspapers."

"But you kept seeing her," Dane said slowly.

"Sheila was important to me in a way which I doubt I
could make anyone understand." His father spoke with
difficulty. "Anyway, I kept sending this dirty hound,
whoever he is, the thousand a month until I was arrested. Naturally, after that he had no further hold over me,
and I stopped paying him. I haven't heard a word about
it since."

"Do you have any of the notes you received?"

"I got just the first one—the one like this, Mr. Queen.
I burned it."

Ellery brooded. "Dane, let's go over the ground
again, in the light of this new information. You left
Sheila before ten o'clock that night. You left her alive.
You didn't show up at your parents' apartment until after midnight. All right. What did you do in those two
hours?"

"I took a little walk first, to cool off. I was horrified at myself, at what I'd almost done. I knew I must have hurt her badly, then I'd run as if I'd murdered her. Finally I decided to go back—"

"You went back?" cried Ellery. Dane's father and Judy were open-mouthed.

"I'm on one hell of a spot, hey?" Dane said with a wry smile. "That's what I did, all right. I figured I owed her an explanation, the story of these rages, to ask her forgiveness if nothing else. So I went back to the building—"

"Did anyone see you?"

"I don't believe so, but I can't be sure."

"Go on."

"I took the elevator up to the penthouse and stood before her door. I raised my hand—I actually raised it —to ring her bell. And . . . I couldn't. I couldn't bring myself to. To ring it, or knock, or use my key, or anything. I chickened out. I couldn't face her."

Oddly, he addressed this last to Judy in a pleading way, as if soliciting her understanding. Her face softened.

"Dane, pay attention. This could be important. You say you took a short walk, then returned to the penthouse—at least to her vestibule. Think now. How long were you gone? Can you tell me?"

"I'm afraid not."

"No idea at all?"

"If I had to guess, I'd say I was gone about fifteen minutes."

"Then it's possible you were outside Sheila's door at 10:23, the time she was shot."

"I suppose so."

"Level with me, Dane. If I'm to help you, I need straight answers. Did you hear a shot from inside the apartment?"

"No. I'd remember if I did."

"I doubt if a shot could be heard, Mr. Queen," the elder McKell said. "The apartments are solidly soundproofed."

Ellery murmured, "Dane stood outside that penthouse apartment just about the time Sheila was shot. Do you see what that means? In all likelihood, you were

142

standing in that vestibule *while the killer was inside.*
Didn't you see or hear anything? How long did you
stand there?"

Dane shook his head. "A very short time. I couldn't
ring or knock, so I went away. I didn't hear or see anything at all."

"You went away. Where?"

"Walked some more."

"Did anyone see you leave? Did you meet anyone you
knew, Dane? Say, in the building?"

"I can't remember anybody. I was in a fog. I do recall
being in a movie theater—"

"That's something," his father exclaimed. "Which
movie theater, son?"

"I don't know. Some neighborhood house. Probably
around Lexington or somewhere."

"What was the title of the picture?"

"How should I know? I tell you I was half off my
rocker!" Dane was growing angry. "I sat there watching
a Western, I remember that, in color, all the fixings, but
when the shooting started and the bodies began flying
around I got up, sick to my stomach, and walked out.
And back to the house and apartment. That's all I can
tell you, Dad."

"Do you have the ticket stub, son?"

"I've looked for it in all my suits. I can't find it. Must
have thrown it away. Who holds on to movie theater
ticket stubs?"

"None of this matters in the least," Ellery said,
frowning. "The essential fact is that Dane was at the
door of the penthouse just about the time the murder
was committed. What difference does it make where he
went afterward?"

There was silence. Ellery began to pull at an invisible
beard; his eyes went perceptibly far, far away. Dane, his
father, Judy, sat uncomfortably still while he reflected.
A truck backfired somewhere, startling them. A dressing
cart clashed by in the corridor. Someone laughed. In the
distance a police siren went off.

After a long time Ellery returned from wherever he
had been. "All right, that's past," he said slowly.
"What's the present situation? First, the blackmailer.
His identity? Well, there have been two blackmailing

143

letters of which we know, each demanding $2,000 down and $1,000 a month thereafter. Each has specified that the payments were to be in $20 bills. Each has been written in block capitals—yours was in pencil, too, Mr. McKell?—and each used the alias 'Mr. I. M. Ecks,' care of General Delivery, main post office. And so on. The similarities are too striking to be coincidence. I agree with you, Mr. McKell, both blackmail notes were written by the same person. So—we're dealing with a single blackmailer."

A touch of color had invaded Ellery's face, paled by several months of exile from the sun.

"The obvious question is: Having a killer at large on the one hand, and a blackmailer at large on the other, what connection—if any—exists between the two?"

"Why, that's so, isn't it?" said Judy thoughtfully. "I didn't think of that."

"A connection very probably exists. The blackmailer's hold on Dane is based on his possession of the original of the letter Sheila Grey wrote just before she was killed. How did the blackmailer get hold of the letter? Well, let's see if we can reconstruct what must have happened on the night of the shooting."

They were sitting forward in their chairs now. Ellery went on deliberately.

"Dane and Sheila had a bitter quarrel. He began to choke her, caught himself in time, ran out of the apartment. He left her alive. A very few minutes later you, Mr. McKell, arrived. You were there just about long enough for Miss Grey to ask you to leave, which you did. That was a few minutes past ten o'clock. It has not been challenged by anyone, through two trials, and we can accept it as a fact, that the shot the precinct officer heard over the phone was the shot that killed Sheila Gray; and the time of the shot, the officer noted officially, was 10:23 P.M. According to the medical examiner's finding, she died instantly. The conclusion has to be that she wrote the letter about Dane, intended for the police, between a few minutes past ten—your departure, Mr. McKell—and 10:23."

"We've been all through that," said Dane impatiently.

"We may have to go through it a great many more times before you're out of the woods, Dane," Ellery said dryly. "Now, then. The first officers on the scene, the radio car men, arrived at the penthouse within minutes of the fatal shot. From their arrival forward, the police were in charge of the premises. Yet, in spite of the police search, which we have a right to assume was thorough, especially in view of the sensational nature of Sheila's letter, the letter was not found. Conclusion: the letter was no longer there. Further conclusion: it had been taken from the premises before the arrival of the police. Still further conclusion: since we know it came into possession of the blackmailer, the weight of the evidence is on the side of the blackmailer's having found it. He found it, he photographed it, he still has it.

"How did the blackmailer come to find it?"

Ellery shrugged. "Who was the one person we know was in the penthouse between the time Sheila finished writing the letter and the time the police got there? Her murderer. Unless we are willing to credit the theory that between the departure of the murderer—which could not have been before 10:23—and the arrival of the police a mere handful of minutes later, still another person—the blackmailer—came on the scene, searched it, found the Grey letter, and left without being detected by anyone, including the police . . . unless, as I say, we are willing to credit a theory so far-fetched, only one conclusion is permissible: *the murderer of Sheila and the finder of the letter—that is, the blackmailer—are one and the same.*

"If we can lay our hands on this mysterious blackmailer, then, Mr. Ecks," Ellery said softly, "we'll have caught the killer of Sheila Grey. That job is too much for amateurs. We'll need professional help, and that means my father."

"You can't do that, Mr. Queen!" cried Judy.

"I agree with Judy. It would mean revealing the contents of Sheila's letter." Ashton McKell shook his head. "And that would plunge my son deep into the case, Mr. Queen."

"All I intend to tell my father," Ellery said, "is that Dane is being blackmailed, not the basis for it. Leave Inspector Richard Queen to an expert, won't you? I know how to handle him; I've had enough practice! Agreed? Dane?"

145

Dane was quiet. Then he threw up his hands. "I'm ready to be guided by whatever you say, Mr. Queen."

Judy Walsh came away from the hospital meeting in a sweet euphoria. How poor Dane must have suffered! How unreasonably, blindly female she had been! But from now on . . . ah, things would be different between them. She was so very sure her love, her compassion, her active assistance, would help him overcome the frightening problem of his rages. If necessary, she would get him to seek psychiatric help. And then, with the homicidal blackmailer caught and eliminated from their lives, the case would be closed forever, Sheila Grey would become an ebbing if always unpleasant memory, they would find peace, would carve out new lives for themselves . . . in short, they would live happily ever after.

"So Dane McKell is being blackmailed," said Inspector Queen, "and I'm not to ask any questions about it. Is that it, Ellery?"

"That's it," and his son beamed.

"Well, you just forget it. I don't buy blind pigs in pokes, or whatever the blasted saying is. Even from you."

"Dad, have I ever steered you wrong?"

"Thousands of times," the Inspector replied, "thousands."

"Name one."

"Sure. There was the time—"

"Never mind," Ellery said. "Dad, listen to me this once, will you? If I weren't laid up I wouldn't even bother you with it. It's merely a case of laying a trap for a blackmailer."

"What's Dane being blackmailed about?" demanded the old gentleman.

"I can't tell you now."

"It's in connection with the Grey case, of course."

"I tell you I can't. You'll know the whole story later. Don't you trust me any longer?"

"I don't trust myself these days," the Inspector said with gloom. "The D.A. and I have practically stopped talking to each other. I've never *seen* such a case."

"You want to settle it?"

"Of course I want to settle it!"

"Then do it my way, Dad."

"You're blackmailing *me!"*

"Right," Ellery said cheerfully. "Then it's a deal? You post your men at the main post office, have them watch the General Delivery window. The postal authorities will co-operate. They'll give your men the tip-off when the fellow shows up—"

"And suppose they make a mistake?" the old man asked sourly. "And suppose the city is sued for false arrest, with me in the middle of it? How do I defend myself for ordering an arrest without having seen the evidence that a crime may have been committed? What do I do, refer them to you? Nothing doing, Ellery."

But Ellery had an answer for everything this morning. A security guard from the McKell organization, one of the scores employed to watch the McKell warehouses, docks, factories, and other buildings, could be assigned to watch the post office along with the regular police. When the trap was sprung, this privately employed guard would make a citizen's arrest, with the police staying out of it. If the arrest were resisted, the police could then step in, restrain and compel—their duty at any time—with impunity.

Inspector Queen listened in silence. He was sorely, sorely tempted. The Grey case had been his headache since the discovery of the body; it was turning into a migraine. If it was true, as Ellery had hinted, that the blackmailer in question might turn out to be the slayer of Sheila Grey, one Richard Queen was off the hook. He might even get a departmental citation out of it.

In the end the old man yielded, as Ellery had known he would.

So on the next day the lobby of the great post office behind Pennsylvania Station was sprinkled with plain-clothesmen and detectives from Inspector Queen's command, along with Ashton McKell's private guard. The postal authorities had agreed to co-operate. The package containing $2,000 in $20 bills (instructions of "Mr. I. M. Ecks," to the contrary notwithstanding, *not* unmarked) had been made up, mailed, had arrived, was waiting to be picked up.

The trap was baited and laid.

It was never sprung.

No one showed up to claim the package.

Whether the blackmailer had spotted the police waiting to arrest him, or he had been scared away by his own guilty imaginings, there was no way of telling; the fact was, the bait lay beyond the General Delivery window, unnibbled.

So passed December 28th.

On the morning of December 29th . . .

The real fireworks had occurred late the night before, in the hospital room of one Ellery Queen. The Inspector had barged in long after visiting hours, angrily flushed, triumphant, and loaded for bear.

"I don't care a curse what your rules are," he had assured the indignant night nurse, flourishing his inspector's shield under her nose. "And don't any of you Florence Nightingales dare interrupt us even if you hear me strangling your patient, which he bloody well deserves!" And he secured the door with the back of a chair.

Ellery was reading in bed.

"Dad?" He peered into the gloom. "You got him?"

"Listen, sonny-boy," Inspector Queen said, hauling a chair over and snatching the book out of Ellery's hand, "I'll tell you what I've got. I've got heartburn and a bellyful, mostly of you. You can't tell me the basis of the blackmail, hey? The hell you can't! You don't have to. I'm wise to the whole smelly business now. You ought to be ashamed of yourself, keeping a thing like that from your own father—"

"What," asked Ellery in an injured tone, "is this remarkable performance all about?"

"I'll tell you what it's about!"

"Keep your voice down, Dad. This is a hospital."

"It's about your precious Dane McKell! You know what happened this evening?"

"That's what I've been trying, unsuccessfully so far, to find out."

"What happened is that we received a Special Delivery envelope at headquarters is what *happened*. Full of interesting stuff, yes, sir. All kinds of reference material. Most fascinating of the bunch was a letter addressed to the police, in Sheila Grey's handwriting, that she wrote the night she was knocked off. How do you like those apples?"

"Oh," said his son.

"And ooh and ah! You knew all about it, didn't you? But not a word about it to me. Your own father. In charge of the damn case. Not a *word*. I have to find out about it from an anonymous donor."

"Dad," said his son.

"Don't Dad me! All right, I know what you're going to say. This stuff came from the blackmailer—"

"And how," Ellery asked placatingly, "did he get it?"

"How should I know? I don't care! The point is, he got it, and he sent it to us, and now *I've* got it, and those McKells are going to rue the day! Especially that—that Hamlet-pussed pal of yours, Dane!"

"Whoa, slow down," the son said. "You're not as young as you used to be. Give this to me in something like intelligible sequence, will you, Inspector?"

"Glad to oblige," chortled his father. "Here's the way we dope it. First of all this blackmailer, who calls himself I. M. Ecks, doesn't show—probably spotted the trap. He knows he can't hope to collect a penny any more. So he sends the blackmail material to us—out of revenge, disappointment, malice; it doesn't matter why. It's no good to him. But it's just what the doctor ordered for us.

"So. We now shift gears in the Grey case, and for the first time—armed with *real* evidence—we're on the right track. We were wrong about the parents, but there's no mistake this time. This Dane is *it*. The third McKell turns out to be the right one. And there'll be no acquittal in *his* trial."

"You're still not telling me anything," Ellery said fretfully. "What have you got besides the Grey letter? You realize that all the letter does is establish that Sheila Grey was still alive when Dane left her—"

149

"Oh, it establishes a lot more than that, my son. But let's not pick over picayunes. Let's tackle this scientifically. You want science?"

"I want science."

"I'll give you science. How's this? We've got a witness, a *reliable* witness, who saw your Dane come *back* to the penthouse."

Ellery was quiet.

"No reaction?" chomped the old man. "That tells me you knew about that, too. Thank God I raised you to be a rotten liar. Ellery, I don't understand. Withholding information like that! How did you find out?"

"I didn't say I found out anything."

"Come *on*, son."

"All right," Ellery said suddenly. "Dane told me. Himself. Would he have done that if he had anything to be afraid of?"

"Sure he would," said the Inspector. "If he was very smart. If he figured it would come out sooner or later anyway. Well, if you know that, you know he took the elevator right up there. Want to know what time? Or do you know it? Don't bother. It was 10:19, my son, when he stepped into that elevator—10:19 P.M. and going *up* —*four minutes* before she stopped that bullet, Dane McKell was zooming up to the penthouse! My witness watched the elevator dial swing right up there from the lobby, no stops."

"I suppose it was the doorman."

"You suppose correctly. We had a tough time prying the truth out of John Leslie tonight, but we cracked him. For some reason that escapes me he feels loyalty to the McKells. Well, we knocked it out of him. I'm not taking anybody's crud in this case any more. I've *had* it."

"Did he tell you anything else?"

"Yes, he told us something else. He told us that Dane McKell's been visiting that penthouse with great regularity. That's one your friend almost slipped over on us. With his old man involved with Sheila, we never pictured the son was, too. We did a quick check tonight, enough to tell us he'd been running around with her in a way that means only one thing. So there's the motive. He was having an affair with her, but this lady's affairs seem to have been jumpy transactions—the man was

150

here today and gone tomorrow. She must have given your friend Dane the old gate and he wouldn't or couldn't take it. So blam! first he starts to strangle her, has second thoughts, leaves, then comes back in about a half hour and lets her have it with the gun his mother thoughtfully loaded with live ammo."

"And the blackmailer?" Ellery asked, not strongly.

"I know all about the blackmailer. You'll say he had to have been on the premises about the same time in order to have got his mitts on the letter. Right. I agree. How about *at* the same time?"

"What do you mean?" Ellery asked, puzzled.

"I mean Dane McKell hooked that letter after he whopped Sheila with the blaster. That this whole business of blackmail is so much happy dust he's flung into our eyes!"

"No," Ellery said. "No, that would have been pure idiocy. That would mean *he* sent you the original of the letter. To accomplish what? His own arrest for murder, when before that you didn't even suspect him? You'll have to do better than that, Dad."

"Maybe he felt the collar tightening around his neck. *I* don't know. Anyway, it's not our worry, it's his. You know, my son? We've got a case, and this one is going to stick."

So on the morning of December 29th Sergeant Velie and the speechless Detective Mack, herded by Inspector Queen in person, visited the apartment of the three McKells while they were at breakfast (it always seemed to come, Dane afterward thought, at breakfast) and Ashton McKell said frigidly, "Don't you people know any other family in this city? What is it this time?"; and Inspector Queen showed his dentures in a feral grin and said, "I have a warrant for the arrest of Dane McKell."

IV. The Fourth Side

DANE

The grand jury, the arraignment, the bail—it was beginning to feel like a well-used merry-go-round; as Dane said, "Here we go again."

Some uniformed policeman in the corridor were discussing him as if he were not present, or were made of wood.

"Think he'll beat it, too?"

"Well, the D.A.'s got two strikes against him now, the father and mother. One more whiff and he's out. He can't afford to strike out."

"Nah, the son will beat it the way his daddy and ma did. I'll bet money on it."

"They've got the dough to do it."

"I don't think so. Not this time. This time he can paper the hot seat with his money."

Dane passed on, not comforted.

Part of the carrousel by now was the council of war in the hospital room, with Ellery dourly presiding. The medical conferees had decided at the last moment to keep him in the hospital an extra few days until he became accustomed to crutches. He was not comforted, either.

He had accepted the contract, so to speak, but he was not exactly bursting with confidence. This time he was profoundly certain that the same *modus* which had saved Dane's parents would not work. There could be no alibi for Dane. At the critical moment, where Ashton had been in an identifiable bar, talking to an identifiable bartender; where Lutetia had been talking over the telephone on a coast-to-coast TV hook-up . . . by his own admission Dane was virtually on the scene of the shooting, standing before the penthouse apartment door, separated from slayer and slain by the thickness of the door panel. And in that tiny penthouse elevator foyer he had been standing alone and unobserved—indeed, unobservable, for there were no windows in the foyer. Consequently, there could be no witness to his allegation that he had simply stood there for a few moments and then left without entering the apartment.

No, this time they would have to do what they should have done from the outset, Ellery said.

"I'd have done it if I'd been on my toes and feet," he told Dane, Ashton McKell, and Judy. "The only way to get Dane off—the only sure way—is to find Sheila's killer.

"If we had been able to do that when you were under indictment, Mr. McKell, we would have been spared all that followed, including Mrs. McKell's ordeal, and now Dane's. Well, we couldn't; I'll stop bemoaning it and get down to cases."

Ellery shifted his aching legs to an equally uncomfortable position. "Up to now we've been working from the outside in, trying to prove why the accused couldn't have done it—the negative approach. This time we've got to work from the inside out. Positively. Agreed?"

They followed, they nodded, they agreed. But without spirit. They all felt fagged. Judy Walsh's eyes were a chronic swollen red; crying had become part of her life, like brushing her teeth. She sat clinging to Dane's arm as if she were pulling him back from the edge of a cliff.

"The beginning, the source of everything, is Sheila herself. 'In my end is my beginning,' as Mary Queen of Scots said." (Tactfully, Ellery did not mention the circumstances under which she had said it.) "Where did Sheila begin? Her business, for example. Didn't one of you, when we were first looking at her fashion designs, mention that she'd started her designing career in partnership?"

"With a man named Winterson." Ashton McKell nodded. "Elisha Winterson. I recall Sheila's saying he was still in New York."

"Good. Then we start with him. See if you can't get him to visit me here this afternoon."

"I'll have him here at the point of a gun, if necessary."

154

Such measures were not required. Elisha Winterson was highly flattered to have Ashton McKell himself come calling for him at Countess Roni's, the Fifth Avenue fashion salon with which he was associated.

The countess seemed flattered, too. "Such a dreadful business!" she exclaimed in her strongly Italian accent; she had been in the United States for over twenty years, and it had been a struggle to retain the sound of Rome, but she had been victorious. "Poor Sheila. And this persecution of your family, Mr. McKell. Lish, you must help. Don't waste a moment!"

As Ramon drove them to the hospital, Elisha Winterson talked and talked. He was a small dapper man with a bald head, the top of which was caved in, so that from above, as Countess Roni (who was six feet tall) had once remarked, his head looked like one of the craters of the moon.

"Roni is very sweet and *simpatico*," Winterson chattered. "You know, she's not Italian at all, although she lived in Italy for a long time. That's where she met poor old Sigi. I saw his patent of nobility myself, yards and yards of moldy old parchment dripping with seals, Holy Roman Empire, defunct, 1806, but as I say, who cares? I most certainly don't. As for Sheila—"

Ashton McKell said, "Mr. Winterson, would you mind not going into that until Queen can question you?"

Winterson's sunken-domed head shot around. "Queen? What queen is that?"

"Ellery Queen."

"The author? He's helping you? Well, of course, Mr. McKell, just as you say." He seemed torn between awe and a private joke. "I'll stay bottled up till he uncorks me."

In the hospital room Elisha Winterson babbled away, lit Turkish cigarets, bombarded Ellery with praise, and then presented himself for uncorking. "I understand you want to ask me about Sheila Grey, Mr. Queen. Fire when ready."

"Tell me all about your association with her. How,

155

when, where you met her, how you came to go into partnership, and so on."

"I met her in 1956," Winterson said. "It was at one of those little parties that Roni—that's Countess Roni, the designer I'm working with now—is famous for. I was, if I may say so, rather widely known. But Sheila was already well on her way to being an international figure in high fashion. So I was flattered when she suggested we go into business together. I mean—"

"This was in 1956?"

"Early in 1957. I mean, Sheila could have had almost anyone in the profession as her partner. That girl had flair, impeccable taste. And a sense of timing, which is *very* important. She did all her own sketching, too. It was a great break for me. Not only career-wise, by the way. She was the most fascinating woman I'd ever met. I was in love with her even before we established The House of Grey."

He would be utterly candid with them, Winterson said (glancing at Judy): he was very much the ladies' man, he said with a laugh. "You wouldn't think it, looking at me." But discriminating; he was no old lecher. He wanted Sheila and he pursued her "in my own fashion" (contriving to leave the impression that his "fashion" was immensely subtle, a sort of secret process which he had no intention of giving away). At first their relationship was all work and no play. He had almost given up hope that it would ever be anything else when, one night, without preliminary, she took him as her lover.

"That's the way it was with Sheila," Winterson said with a wistful half-smile. "Nothing but camaraderie for months, then—bango! if you'll forgive the expression, Miss Walsh. No one ever sold Sheila Grey a bill of goods unless she was absolutely ready to buy. She was one of the world's shrewdest shoppers where men were concerned. And then she kept it a one-man-at-a-time affair." Dane found his fists curling with hatred of this smug little dressed-up troglodyte.

The House of Grey had its first official showing that year, 1957. It created a sensation abroad as well as in the United States. "Lady Sheila—that was her name for our first collection—put us right up there on top."

"I mean to ask you about that—" Ellery began.

"Lady Sheila? It was Sheila's idea to call each year's collection by some sort of name, and she chose the Lady Sheila label for 1957. Sheila, by the way, wasn't her own name."

"It wasn't?" the McKells cried out together.

"Her original first name was Lillian, and her last name was spelled G-r-a-y. When we organized The House of Grey, it was her decision to change the *a* to an *e* in *Grey;* and when the Lady Sheila collection was such a smash hit, she had her name legally changed from Lillian G-r-a-y to Sheila G-r-e-y."

"That was also in 1957?"

"Yes, Mr. Queen."

"How long did your association last?"

"Which association?"

"Both."

"Well." Winterson looked coy. "We were lovers for just a few months. I was very happy and assumed she was, too. We were compatible, you know?" Dane closed his eyes. The picture of this scrubbed little creature in Sheila's arms was almost too much to bear. "We went about together everywhere, enjoyed our love and labors with the gusto of teenagers—oh, it was marvelous. Then . . .

"I shan't forget that day." Winterson was no longer smiling. "It was just before she began designing the 1958 collection, the Lady Nella. I'd worked up some roughs and brought them into her office—laid them on her desk and stooped over to kiss her." He had turned quite pink. "She drew back and kept on with her work. I was upset, and asked her what was the matter. She looked up and said as calmly as if she were talking about the weather, 'It's over between us, Lish. From now on we're partners, nothing more.' Just like that. No transition. The way she'd begun."

He had asked her why, what he had done. " 'You haven't done anything.' " she had told him. " 'It's just that I don't want you any more.' "

Winterson shrugged, but the pink remained. "That's the way it was with Sheila. All or nothing. When she gave herself, it was fully. When she got tired of it— slam. Shut, locked and bolted the door . . . Well, that's the way she was. But I wasn't. I was in love with

157

her; I wasn't able to turn it off like a faucet. I'm afraid it became a strain for both of us. Of course, we couldn't go on. We split up in a matter of months—three months, I think it was."

She had bought Winterson out and become sole proprietor of The House of Grey. "Of course, my disappearance from the business made absolutely no difference to its continuing success," he said, with a remarkable absence of bitterness. "I've never had any illusions about myself, especially by contrast with a great designer like Sheila. She went on to become one of the world's top *couturières*. Rolling in money. Not that money ever meant much to her."

"Let's go back a bit, Mr. Winterson," Ellery suggested. "You remarked that she was a one-man-at-a-time woman. Are you sure of that?"

Elisha Winterson was taking a long drag on his Spahi. He let the thick white smoke dribble out of his mouth before he replied. "I'm sure," he said, "and I'll tell you why I'm sure." His little face suddenly turned foxy. "After she kicked me out of her bed, I kept wondering who was taking my place. I'm not especially proud of myself now—it was a caddish trick—but you know, a lover scorned . . ." He laughed. "I hired a private detective. I even remember his name. Weirhauser. Face all angles, like Dick Tracy. Had an office on 42nd Street, off Times Square. He watched her for me, and I kept getting full reports—what she did, where she went, with whom. There wasn't anyone. She hadn't ditched me for another man. She'd simply ditched me, period.

"Later that year," said Elisha Winterson, "there *was* another man. I'm certain that shortly after they met he was parking his shoes where I'd been parking mine, if you'll pardon the crudity."

"Who was he?" Ellery asked.

"Well." Winterson ran the tip of his tongue along his lips. "A gentleman never tells, they say. But these are unusual circumstances, I take it? If it will help you, Mr. Queen—"

"It might."

Winterson looked around at his silent audience. What he saw made him go on quickly. Sheila had begun to advertise widely, he said. She had selected to do her advertising the Gowdy-Gunder Agency, because of its familiarity with the world of fashion.

"At the same time The House of Grey hired a business manager, a production manager, began to do its own manufacturing, moved out of the rather poky little place we'd had in the East 50s and into the Fifth Avenue salon. Naturally, Sheila Grey was a plum to the agency people, and they turned their Brightest Young Man over to her account.

"Like catnip to a cat," Winterson said grimly, "though I'm sure the experience did him a world of good. His name was Allen Bainbridge Foster, and she ate him up hide, hair, and whiskers. By the end of the year—"

"Allan as in Edgar Allan Poe?" Ellery had reached for a pad and was taking notes.

"No, Allen with an *e*."

"Bainbridge Foster?"

"That's right. As I started to say, by the end of the year she'd had enough of Mr. Foster, and she gave him his walking papers, too."

"Were you still having her watched, Mr. Winterson?" Ellery asked, not without a touch of malice.

"Oh, no, I'd called Weirhauser off long before that. But Sheila and I had a lot of friends and acquaintances in common, like Countess Roni and so on, so I heard all the gossip. You know how it is."

"I do now. And after Foster?"

"I can virtually vouch for her lovers—three of them —in the next four years. Sheila was without shame where *l'amour* was concerned. She didn't care a button about her reputation, I mean personally, and while she certainly didn't go around flaunting her affairs, neither did she take any pains to be discreet. None of this hurt The House of Grey in the least, by the way. After all, she wasn't designing altar pieces for churches. On the contrary, it seemed to add to her glamour. It attracted men to her salon in herds."

"You say you know of three others in the next four years. Who were they, have you any idea?"

"Of course. Jack Hurt was one."

"John Francis Hurt III, the auto racer?"

"That's the one. Jack made no secret of it. He carried

159

Sheila's photo in his wallet for good luck. He'd show it to you at the drop of a flag. 'I'm crazy about this little girl,' he'd say. I'm sure Sheila didn't go for him because of his wit. But Jack was muscled like a puma—all male animal. She used to go down into the grease pits at the speedway after him; absolutely gone on him. Then one day, as Jack came roaring in from Lap Eighty-nine to get his lube job or his water changed or whatever they do to the racing cars in the pits—lo! no Sheila. Just changed her mind in mid-lap and went on home. He didn't pine very long, I must say. Latched onto some little blonde who embroidered his name on her jacket, poor slobby-gob, and I believe married her shortly afterward."

"That's Jack Hurt the Three," said Ellery. "Who was his successor?"

"After Hurt? Ronald Van Vester of the veddy high society Van Vesters, who live on the interest of their interest. Don't know where Sheila spotted him, but she did start ponying up on polo"—Winterson tittered at his little jest—" and before you knew it he was making eyes at her. Well, one hoof in the doorway was all Miss Sheila needed, and there was Master Ronny on the line. But I suppose the smell of horse manure soon palled on her. Exit Ronny.

"Next there was . . . let me see." The ineffable Elisha tapped his teeth with a glittering fingernail. "Oh, yes! Some character named Odonnell. The stage actor. Edgar? Edmond? I don't recall, because nobody ever called him by his first name except in the programs. You must remember him, Mr. Queen, all smoldering black eyes and hatchet profile. First man to play Hamlet according to the Method, after which no one called him anything but Hamlet Odonnell."

"You said three in *four* years."

Winterson explained that he had spent all of 1961 abroad, and so had been out of touch. "What happened while I was catching up on what Paris and Rome were doing I have no idea. She could have been having her fling with the Assistant Commissioner of Sanitation for all I know. Hamlet was the lucky man in 1962, when I got back. And since then . . ." Winterson paused.

The silence spread like ink. Dane was looking as if he were about to throw up. Ashton McKell looked deathly ill. All this, then, was new to both of them, Ellery thought. As for Judy, she was grasping the arms of her chair as if they were the rails of a chute-the-chutes car at the top of the trestle.

"I suppose I ought to have realized that, sooner or later, Sheila Grey would come to a nasty end," Winterson said finally. "And yet . . . she was so utterly *charming* when she was in love. She needed love. It was the fuel, I think, that made her go, that and her career . . . God, what a waste. She had the world at her feet."

Suddenly he was no longer a ridiculous little frou-frou of a man with a caved-in head. His face was the mask of tragedy. Ellery thought: He's still in love with her.

Winterson jumped to his feet. "If there's anything else I can tell you, here's my card. By all means call on me. Goodbye, Miss Walsh, Mr. McKell." To Dane he said, "I wish you all the luck."

Ashton said, "My car—"

"Thank you, but I believe I'll walk for a bit." And, nodding all around, his smile perfunctory, he darted from the hospital room, leaving the memory of his twisted face and the sluggish overhand of his Turkish tobacco.

"And that was something Mr. Winterson had to get out of his system," Ellery remarked. "I wonder how many years he's unconsciously hunted for the opportunity."

"He was *disgusting*." Judy made a face.

"It was also a rich vein, and we mustn't let it go untapped. I'll have to depend on one or all of you to be my eyes, ears, and legs."

"Tell us what you want done, Mr. Queen," said the elder McKell.

"I want all four of the men Elisha Winterson named to be checked for alibis for the night of September 14th. No, not four—five. Winterson, too. Yes, begin with Winterson. Then Foster, then"—he glanced at his notes —"Hurt, then Van Vester, then Odonnell."

Dane was already helping Judy into her coat.

161

"I'll get on it right away, Mr. Queen," Ashton Mc-Kell said. "Hire some Pinkerton people—a squad of them, if necessary."

"Good. And let me have their reports as they come in."

At last he was alone, and in the way he had of letting himself go mentally—like an athlete deliberately relaxing his muscles, muscle by muscle, on a training table —Ellery sank himself deeper and deeper into thought. There was something here . . . something . . . He fanned the air to dissipate Winterson's smog trail, and as he did so his eye fell on the fanning card, and he saw that it was the personal card Winterson had handed him on departing. Idly, he read it.

And Ellery's face went white as the card itself.

Was it possible that . . . ?

As his color returned, he kept mumbling to himself something about a fool and his folly.

After that, he could hardly wait for the reports.

As the reports came in from the detective agency, Ashton McKell sent them to Ellery, who arranged them in piles on his writing desk: Winterson, Foster, Hurt, Van Vester, Odonnell.

He analyzed.

On the night of September 14th:

—Winterson had been in an Air France plane en route to Rome. The French press at Orly had interviewed him on his opinions of current fashion, recorded his polite platitudes, photographed him getting on the plane. The Italian press had performed a similar task when he got off in Rome.

—Foster had been in Chicago. He had changed jobs shortly after his breakup with Sheila Grey and moved, with his wife and two children, to the Windy City, where he had been living ever since. At the time of the murder

he had been attending a meeting of a bra and founda-
tion garment high command, representing his advertising agency, in the company of a roomful of vice-presi-
dents.

—John F. "Jack" Hurt III was no longer among the
automobile-fancying population. In 1961, in a stock-car
race in Florida, his machine had hurtled out of control
on a turn; when he was removed from the flaming
wreckage he was dead.

—Van Vester was also dead. He had been drowned
the previous year in a boating accident off the Florida
Keys.

—Eddwin "Hamlet" Odonnell had been in England,
playing the role he was most noted for in repertory. At
the moment of the murder in New York he was giving
an imitation of Elizabeth Taylor as Cleopatra at an all-
night party in London, in the presence of several dozen
more or less sober stars of British stage and screen.
Dame Vesta Morisey herself vouched for him.

Then whoever had shot Sheila Grey to death, it had
not been one of these five former lovers.

But by this time Ellery knew it could not have been
one of them, anyway.

When Dane visited the hospital on the morning of December 31st, he found Ellery's room in confusion.
Clothes and books were everywhere, suitcases lay open,
flower vases were being emptied, and Ellery was hop-
ping around on his aluminum crutches in a sort of joyous grouch.

"Are you checking out after all?" Dane asked. "I
thought you said the doctor had changed his mind."

"I changed his mind back," Ellery snarled. "I'm
damned if I'm going to stay in this lazaret for another
year. I think they're secretly burning punk in thanksgiv-
ing for getting rid of me. If I could only maneuver
gracefully on these cursed hobblesticks! Oops!—sorry,
Kirsten."

He almost knocked the resplendent Swedish nurse
over, and in trying to catch her he all but fell himself.
Dane sprang in to avert further broken bones.

"Mr. *Queen*," the lovely nurse said. "You must not the crutches use so! *This* way . . ."

"I'm tired," Ellery said. And sat down. "By the way, Dane, tonight being what the Scotch call hogmanay, I'm throwing a little party at the apartment—"

"Whose?"

"Mine. Kirsten, do you remember what I said about the time when they cut the concrete pants off me?"

"Oh, so bad, I cannot come," the nurse said, blushing. "Sture, his ship comes in. We go together tonight, you see."

"Who's Sture?" demanded Ellery.

She murmured a word in Swedish. "Oh, my boy friend—no, yes, my fiancé. He is second mate. Now we go back to Sweden and he gets yob in ship company office. We will marry." And, scarlet, she fled.

"And a good thing, too," Ellery said gloomily. "Having to occupy the same living space with that goddess day after day without being able to touch her has been almost too much for me to bear. Sture! The Swedes have all the luck. Anyway, I wasn't going to invite Kirsten to my New Year's Eve party. That's strictly for our little in-group. I can count on you-all? Good. Now how about helping me pack?"

The Christmas tree which Ellery had not been able to see on its day of glory was still there when the three McKells and Judy Walsh got to the Queen apartment at 9:30 that night. Partly because of Ellery's delayed Yuletide, partly in the old Knickerbocker tradition of New Year's Day, the McKells had brought gifts. Ramon's arms were full of them.

Inspector Queen was there, too, not altogether gracefully. ("What do you think you're doing?" he had demanded of Ellery. "It isn't bad enough having the parents here, after my part in getting up a case against them, but this son of theirs *I* arrested! It isn't exactly the setup for good social relations." "Dad, trust me." "Trust *you*?" the Inspector had said scathingly. So Ellery had explained; and after that the Inspector helped Ellery ready the apartment; and he was johnny-on-the-spot, dentures grinning, when the McKell party arrived, playing the role of mine host's aging parent like the hardened trouper he was.)

164

"All these gifts," Ellery said, glowing. "Well, I'll be having a New Year's gift for the McKell family myself later tonight. Do you suppose I could borrow Ramon?"

"Of course," said Ashton McKell.

Lutetia said, "How thoughtful of you, Mr. Queen," her anxiety tempered by her supreme confidence that everything would come out right in the end. Sooner or later the law would release her son, as it had released her and her husband. Ashton would see to that. Or Ellery Queen, or both.

"The gift isn't ready, but if Ramon can get back a little after eleven o'clock and run an errand for me . . ."

"Certainly," Ashton said. "Ramon, be back here at, say, 11:15."

The chauffeur said, "Yes, sir," and left.

The presence of the Inspector was something of a damper. Ellery worked hard at playing host. He had put some Elizabethan music on the hi-fi, and he presided like a pitchman over the punch bowl, in which he had prepared a Swedish punch after a convivial recipe given him by one of the hospital doctors. Judy helped him serve the food, which boxed the compass from Peking duck to tiny buckwheat cakes. "There's something of a rite involved in handling the duck," he said. "Mr. McKell, would you be kind enough to carve?" (at which the Inspector growled a very low growl that only his son heard) . . . "Thank you . . . First we take one of these thin little pancakes, or knishes—almost like tortillas, aren't they? . . . spread them with slices of duck . . . green onions . . . the soy sauce, the other sauces . . . roll 'em up . . . tuck in the ends so that the sauce doesn't drip, and fall to. Dane, some more of that hot punch, and skoal to the lot o' yez!"

He told them the story of the very young student nurse who had rushed from a patient's room screaming that his pulse had dropped to 22. The staff had come running, the resident took the pulse over again, laughed, and said, "What did you do, take a fifteen-second count? His pulse is 88." The poor girl had forgotten to multiply by four.

Ellery labored to keep the party going, but the Inspector noticed that he kept glancing at the foyer. Only when the buzzer sounded, and Inspector Queen went to answer the door, did Ellery's anxiety turn to confidence.

"It's Ramon back," the Inspector said.

"Come in, Ramon. A glass of punch?"

The chauffeur glanced at his employer, who nodded. Ramon accepted the steaming red liquid, murmured a health in Spanish, and drank quickly.

"Thank you, sir," he said to Ellery. "Where did you want me to go?"

"I have the address right here." Ellery handed him a card. "Hand them this and they'll give you a package. Try to get back as quickly as possible."

"Yes, sir."

When Ramon left, Ellery commandeered the services of Dane, and Dane came back with a cooler of champagne. Judy turned on the TV set. Times Square was jammed with its New Year's Eve quota of ninnyhammers, as Dane called them—"They're the same folksy folks who clutter up the beaches in summer and jump up and down when the camera turns their way." But no one smiled. The approach of midnight was turning the screw on nerves, as at some impending grim event. And when the door buzzer sounded again, everyone started. But it was only Ramon, back from his errand.

"Not quite midnight," said Ellery. "Thank you, Ramon. Have a glass of champagne with us."

"If it is all right with Mr. McKell—"

"Certainly, Ramon."

The package was tubular, about two feet long. It seemed an odd shape for a gift. Ellery placed it carefully on the mantelpiece.

"There goes the ball on the Times Building," he said. "Fill up!" And as the announcer's countdown reached the tick of midnight, and Times Square roared and fluttered, Ellery lifted his glass. "To the New Year!"

And when they had all drunk, he hobbled over to the television set and turned it off; and he faced them and said, "I promised you a gift. Here it is. I'm ready to name the murderer of Sheila Grey."

Inspector Queen backed off until he was leaning against the jamb of Ellery's study door. Ashton McKell placed both hands on the chair before him, gripping it. Lutetia, in the chair, set her glass down on the table, and it slopped a little. Judy leaned against Dane, who was watching Ellery like a dog.

"Here, once more, and for the last time," said Ellery, "is the timetable of the night of September 14th:

"A few minutes to ten: Dane left Sheila Grey's apartment.

"A few monents later: You, Mr. McKell, arrived. You were sent away about 10:03, almost at once.

"10:19: You, Dane, returned to the building.

"10:23: Sheila Grey was shot to death in her apartment.

"It took the first police officers only a few minutes to reach the scene, since the precinct man was able to put out a call practically at the moment of the shooting, from hearing it over the phone. The radio car men found Sheila Grey dead and began an immediate search of the apartment. They found the revolver. They found the cartridges. They did not find Sheila Grey's note, describing Dane's earlier visit and attack."

The quiet in Ellery's voice did not relax anyone. He seemed unaware of their tension and went on.

"Why didn't the investigating officers, first on the scene, find the note? Obviously, because it had already been removed from the premises. Who removed it? Well, who do we know had it in his possession later, in order to be able to send it to the police? The blackmailer. There was only one way in which the blackmailer could have got hold of the note, and that was by taking it from the Grey apartment.

"Let's tackle the same question temporally," Ellery continued. "When did Sheila write the note? Between Dane's first departure and Ashton's arrival? Not likely: the time that elasped could not have been more than five or six minutes, and some of that time Sheila must have spent recovering from the near-throttling she had suffered. Also, you told me, Mr. McKell, that when you walked into the apartment she was still terribly upset, too upset to have dashed off that longish letter to the police. I think, then, we can rule out the period between Dane's departure and Ashton's arrival as the time when she wrote the letter. She wrote it later.

"When? You left about 10:03, Mr. McKell. Then clearly the note must have been written between 10:03 and 10:23, when she was shot. And it had to have been taken from her workroom between the time she wrote it and the time the police got there. And just as clearly she had not *given* it to the blackmailer, for she addressed it to the police. So again we reach the conclusion: The blackmailer stole it from the apartment. And he could only have stolen it after it was written, which would place him in the apartment around the time of the murder. Let's see if we can narrow this down further."

Someone let out a breath stealthily. The Inspector glanced sharply around, but whoever had done it was again as rigid as the others.

"Who do we *know* now was in the apartment between the writing of the letter and the arrival of the police? The blackmailer. Who else? The murderer. Considering the short time involved, it's a reasonable assumption that blackmailer and murderer were one and the same. But we know something else about this blackmailer-murderer. His attempted blackmailing of Dane was not his first such try. He had had a previous victim—you, Mr. McKell." (And at this Inspector Queen cast such reproach at his son as should have withered him in his tracks had he been looking his father's way; but he was not looking his father's way, he was concentrating on his hypnotized audience.) "I've gone all through the reasoning that identifies each blackmail as the work of the same person, so I won't repeat it.

"The keystone question is: What was the basis for his first blackmail, the blackmailing of Ashton McKell?"

Ellery addressed Lutetia directly, who sat twisted in the chair. "Forgive me if I have to call spades by their right name, Mrs. McKell. But we're dealing with hard facts, and only hard words can describe them.

"The basis of the Ashton McKell blackmailing was *the blackmailer's knowledge of the relationship between Ashton McKell and Sheila Grey.* Who knew or could have known of this relationship? How many persons? Who are they?"

He paused, and into the silence crept the sounds of

New Year revelry from other apartments, the streets.

"I count five. Sheila herself, number one. And would Sheila attempt to blackmail Ashton McKell? Hardly. She admired and respected him." Ashton gripped the back of his wife's chair still harder. "She was willing to foster a communion of spirit, a Platonic friendship, under difficult and sometimes ludicrous circumstances, because of that admiration and respect, quite aside from the misinterpretation society would have placed on the relationship had it become generally known. Sheila certainly did not need money; and had she needed money she would not have had to resort to blackmail—all she had to do was ask for it, and it would have been given to her in full measure, to overflowing—am I right, Mr. McKell?"

"Of course," Ashton said stiffly.

"No, Sheila did not blackmail Ashton McKell. Who else knew of their liaison? Naturally, Ashton. Surely he didn't blackmail himself. Why should he conceivably have done so? It makes no sense. So we eliminate Mr. McKell.

"Who else? You, Mrs. McKell. And subsequently you, Dane. But you are both rich in your own right; even in theory, you would not have to resort to blackmail if you needed money. True, each of you was hurt and resentful of Ashton's conduct, but blackmail is hardly the answer to hurt and resentment. If you wished to punish husband and father for what you conceived to be misconduct, each of you would have chosen a far different course—as in fact each of you did. Blackmail figured in neither.

"So there we are," Ellery said. "Five people knew or could have known about Sheila Grey and Ashton McKell, of whom we have thrown out four as possible blackmailers. The conclusion is inescapable that the fifth person was the blackmailer and, therefore, Sheila Grey's murderer."

"I don't understand," Dane mumbled. "Five? I can't think of a fifth."

"We'll get to that later, Dane. Meanwhile, what else do we know about the identity of this Janus—this individual with two faces, one of blackmail, the other of murder? Curiously, we know a great deal, but to get to it we must dig a rather deep hole.

"Follow me.

"We begin with the gold mine of information deeded to us by Winterson, Sheila's original partner in The House of Grey.

"What did Winterson tell us?

"That Sheila had a succession of lovers, beginning with himself. (If there were earlier ones, as I suppose there were, they are irrelevant to the issue.)

"What else did Winterson say? That Sheila was not her original name. She was born 'Lillian.' When did she change Lillian to Sheila? After the great success of her first important showing, the collection she named Lady Sheila. Why Lady Sheila? Why Sheila at all—*which wasn't her name at the time,* yet which so captivated her that she subsequently took it as her legal name?

"I kept puzzling over this. But the answer came to me in one flash. What's Winterson's given name?"

"Elisha," said Judy, wonderingly.

"Elisha." Ellery waited. No one said anything. "Doesn't any of you see the relationship between 'Elisha' and 'Sheila'?"

Judy cried, *"They're anagrams!"*

"Yes. 'Sheila' is a rearrangement of the letters of 'Elisha.'

"When I saw that, of course," Ellery said, "I also saw that it could have been coincidence. So I went on to her next year's collection, the 1958 one. That one she named Lady Nella. What else was significant in Sheila Grey's life during the year 1958? Well, she had dropped Elisha Winterson both as partner and lover by that time. Did she take a new partner? No. A new lover? Winterson said yes, and named him. Remember his name?"

"Foster, wasn't it?" Dane said.

"His full name."

There was another silence. Then Judy said, "I remember. Something about Edgar Allan Poe . . . Yes! You asked Mr. Winterson how to spell Foster's first name, which was Allen."

"Allen—with an *e*—Bainbridge Foster," Ellery nodded. *"Allen—an anagram of Nella,* the name of her 1958 collection!

"Another coincidence? Let's see."

Winterson had mentioned three other men's names, Ellery pointed out, in identifying Sheila's lovers during the following four years. In 1959 it had been John F. "Jack" Hurt III, speed demon of the raceways. In 1960 it had been the high-society polo player, Ronald Van Vester. Winterson had been abroad during 1961 and was able to suggest no lover's name for that year, but for 1962 he had put the finger on Eddwin Odonnell, the Shakespearean actor.

"John F. Hurt III, 1959," Ellery said. "And the name of Sheila's collection in 1959? Lady Ruth. Hurt —Ruth—*anagrams*.

"Ronald Van Vester, 1960. And the name of the 1960 collection—Lady Lorna D. 'D' for 'Doone'? Not a bit of it. *'Ronald' and 'Lorna D.' are anagrams*.

"The pattern is fixed," said Ellery. "Four years, four anagrams of contemporaneous lovers . . . I must admit that the absence of 1961, the Lady Dulcea year, piqued me, and still does. Because Dulcea—a very strange name indeed, so strange it sounds forced—when you unscramble it trying to make a man's name out of it, peculiarly enough yields the name 'Claude.' Of course, we don't know if there was such a man, or if Sheila was simply taking a sabbatical that year—"

"Wait," Ashton McKell said. "Claude . . . Yes, Sheila spoke a great deal about some Frenchman, a playwright, who came to New York in—when was it? —1961, I think—yes, 1961—to have a play of his produced on Broadway. The way she spoke of him—now that I realize—"

"Claude Claudel," Dane said slowly. "Damn it all, don't tell me he too—"

"1961. Claude. Dulcea." Ellery nodded. "It's too perfectly fitted into the pattern to be coincidental. I think we have a right to assume that Monsieur Claudel was Number One on Miss Grey's 1961 hit parade, for part of the year, anyway."

"But what about 1962?" Inspector Queen could not help asking. He was as fascinated as the others by the anagrammatical pattern.

"Well, according to Winterson, in 1962 the favored man was the actor, Odonnell, whose given name, by which no one ever calls him except on theater programs, is 'Edd'—two *ds*—'win.' Odonnell is always called 'Hamlet' Odonnell, from his tiresome playing of the Shakespearean role. And what was Sheila's 1962 collection named? Lady Thelma. 'Hamlet'—'Thelma.' Anagrams.

"Every lover of Sheila's anagrammatically inspired the name of The House of Grey's collection current during his interregnum. Apparently she preferred to use his Christian name as the basis of the anagram, but she would use the surname if she had to."

And the room was a pocket of silence again in the celebrating world, with the wind outside adding to the noisy merriment. A clock, which had been ticking all along, sounded as if it had just begun. Someone's chair creaked, and someone else breathed a snorty breath. In this emphasized silence a strained voice, Lutetia's said, "Mr. Queen, do go on. Please."

"In a way," Ellery said, "this completes the record. The last complete showing of The House of Grey was the 'Hamlet' Odonnell—Lady Thelma year. But at the time of her death Sheila was working on her new collection. She had drawn roughs and made sketches, and had actually completed at least one design.

"Since collections and lovers go together in Sheila's case, who was her last—her most recent—lover? What man was intimate with her during the past year? Forgive me for becoming personal again, Mr. McKell, but that wasn't you. You fell into a special category in Sheila's life; besides, your name doesn't anagrammatize." Ashton McKell's face was still set in plaster of Paris. "Was it you, Dane? Yes, but only in the most limited of senses, as far as I can gather. You and Sheila had really not had time to establish a meaningful relationship. You may have been on your way to it; but, in any case, whom were you following? Whose place would you have filled? Because there is someone—someone you don't suspect."

Ellery sounded as weary as his audience looked startled.

He reminded them, from Winterson's account and from what Sheila herself had told Dane, that she dropped her lovers as suddenly as she took them. If at the time of Dane's appearance in her life she had already dropped her most recent lover—assuming such an unknown existed—or if he had somehow learned that he was about to be dropped by this unpredictable one-man-at-a-time woman, as she had called herself, then a perfect motive for murder could be expected. Hell might have no fury like a woman scorned, Ellery pointed out, but as a matter of statistical fact more murders of frustrated passion and love-revenge were committed in the United States by men than by women.

"We have one feasible way," he said, "to check the theory that another lover existed in Sheila's life—the lover Dane was in the process of displacing. *Had she named the new collection she was working on at the time of her death?*" Ellery started to rise, but he sank back in the chair with a grimace. "These damned legs of mine," he said. "Ramon, would you mind? The tubular package on the mantelpiece."

The chauffeur brought it to him, and Ellery unwrapped it, disclosing a roll of heavy paper. He unrolled it, glanced over it, nodded, and held it up for all to see.

It was the beautifully finished fashion drawing of a model in a sports outfit. The clothes were sketched in exquisite detail.

"This is the only design Sheila Grey had time to finish," Ellery said. "And it tells us the name Sheila had selected for the collection. Here it is at the bottom: Lady Norma, in black lettering.

"Lady Norma," Ellery went on swiftly, with no sign of weariness now, "and I point out to you that 'Norma' is an anagram of the name of the fifth person who was in a position to know of the Sheila-Ashton rendezvous—the fifth person who, the other four having been eliminated, *must* have been the blackmailer—and Sheila's killer. For who else could have known that Ashton McKell visited Sheila Grey? His chauffeur, who dropped him off at the club Wednesday after Wednesday and picked him up again late every Wednesday night, and who was uniquely situated to suspect the nature of those Wednesday excursions—and to verify them. His chauffeur, who somehow became Dane's predecessor in Sheila's affections and then murdered her for throwing him over—*Dad, watch Ramon!*"

Ramon had backed toward the foyer. His skin had turned a putty color; his nostrils were pinched white with surprise, anger, and fear; the line-up of his teeth glittered in his swarthy face. And as Inspector Queen, Dane, and Ashton McKell closed in on him, Ramon seized a heavy chair, flung it at them, and was gone through the apartment door.

The Inspector half caught the chair; part of it banged against Ashton McKell's legs and tripped him; and Dane tripped over his father. For a moment the three men were an impossible tangle of arms and legs. Then, shouting, the McKells regained their feet and plunged toward the foyer. But Inspector Queen roared, "No! He may be armed! Let him go!" And as they stopped, panting, he said, "He can't get away. I have detectives posted at every exit of the building. He'll run straight into their arms."

Later, over restorative brandy—although Ashton McKell was still shocked by the revelation to regain his natural florid color—Ellery said, "Yes, Ramon, whose name inspired Sheila Grey to label her new collection Norma, was her last lover." Out of pity he did not glance at the elder McKell. "It was Ramon whom she dropped when she became interested in you, Dane, and his Spanish pride brought on a homicidal rage." He forbore to go into the question of Sheila's taste in men, knowing that part of Ashton's shock resulted from the fact that his own chauffeur had been sleeping with the woman of his dreams; her lovers had been a heterogeneous lot, and he supposed that the Spaniard—Ramon *was* handsome in a Mediterranean way—had struck her fancy.

"It was Ramon who came to Sheila's apartment that night, sneaked into the bedroom to get the revolver he knew was in the night-table drawer—forgive me again, but he had had plenty of opportunity to become acquainted with that bedroom—and, entering Sheila's workroom, shot her dead as she sat telephoning the police. It was Ramon, of course, who replaced the phone

174

on the cradle, found Shelia's letter to the police, pocket-ed it, and escaped.

"He took the letter to use for blackmailing Dane; or, if that failed, as it did, to draw suspicion away from himself by pointing it toward Dane . . . as it also did.

"He almost got away with it."

There was very little conversation until someone rapped at the door and Inspector Queen opened it to find Sergeant Velie there, grinning massively.

"You got him, I take it," the Inspector said.

"We got him, Inspector. He's quiet now, being a real good boy. You coming downstairs with us?"

"As soon as I get my coat and hat."

When the door closed on them, as if on signal a bab-ble of exclamation broke out.

"It's over, it's over."

"How can we ever thank you, Mr. Queen?"

"By God, he did it. Mr. Queen—Ellery—"

"This calls for another toast!"

"What a New Year's gift," cried Ashton McKell. "Are there the fixings for another toast?"

Three more bottles of champagne were found in the kitchen. Glasses chimed joyously. After a while, Ashton was singing a song of his college youth. ("Oh, we'll sing of Lydia Pinkham/And her love for the human race,/How she makes her Vegetable Compound,/And the papers publish her face.") And Lutetia hiccupped ever so slightly and burst into slightly raffish laughter; and Judy danced a jig to the humming by the assembled company of "The Irish Washerwoman."

And when Ellery said, "I don't mind telling you that my self-esteem has been restored," it was Lutetia Mc-Kell who cried, "To the armchair detective and his re-stored self-esteem!" and they drank the toast in the last of the champagne, while Ellery smiled and smiled.

The fact that "the chauffeur done it," as the man on the street put it, seemed to take the zing out of the Sheila Grey murder case. It was as if the case-hardened mys-tery buff, reading a new work of fiction, were to follow the red herring through 250 pages and find, on page 251, that the criminal was the butler. Other news began to crowd the Grey case into corners of the front pages, and soon it was being reported on page 6, and beyond.

The McKells dropped out of the news entirely.

It was a wonderful relief. Ashton threw himself back into his business with something very like fury. He had neglected his affairs for a long time, and he was not a man to be satisfied with the work of subordinates. The cocoa bean crop in Ghana, the sugar shipments from Peru, the problem of substitutes for Havana tobacco, the efforts of half a dozen new nations to creat merchant marines—he dealt with such matters like a juggler confident of his prowess. Judy was lunching with him at the office these days because of the heavy work-load he piled on her.

Lutetia was happily back at her charity sewing, even (for the first time in two decades) engaging a seamstress to help her with the backlog of illegitimate layettes.

Dane set out to finish his novel, secretly doubting that it would ever be accomplished. It held too many associations for him of the summer. Summer of probing Sheila, dating Sheila, wooing Sheila, loving Sheila . . . summer of Sheila; he knew it would never be anything else in his mind. Except that it was also the summer of having lost Sheila forever.

Half-heartedly he toyed with the idea of abandoning the novel-in-progress and starting another, but he put it off, promising himself that he would embark on a profitable schedule as soon as the indictment against him was formally dropped. The only word he had had since Ramon's arrest was that his lawyers had procured an indefinite postponement of his trial, pending the quashing of the indictment. But as the days passed and he heard nothing, he grew irritated.

He phoned police headquarters.

At first Inspector Queen, who sounded peculiar, suggested that he get in touch with the district attorney's office. Then suddenly he said, "Maybe it's just as well. Wait, Mr. McKell. As long as you've phoned me—"

"Yes?"

"Some questions have come up. Maybe I'd better discuss them with you. I was intending to call you later, but I guess this is as good a time as any."

"What questions?"

"I'll tell you what," the Inspector said. "I'd like my son to be present. Suppose we make it my apartment at two o'clock, all right?"

Dane showed up with his parents and Judy in tow. "I don't know what this is all about," he said to the Queens, "but I told my father about it, and he seemed to feel that all of us ought to be present."

"I don't know what it's about, either," Ellery said, regarding the Inspector with narrowed eyes. "So, Dad, how about laying it on the line?"

Inspector Queen said, "We've been questioning this Ramon Alvarez day and night for—it seems to me—an eternity. He's a funny one."

"How do you mean, Dad?"

"Well, I've grilled murder suspects by the hundreds in my time, and I've never run across one with just this combination of frankness and mulishness. He's made some important admissions, such as being in the penthouse during the general crime period, but he keeps insisting he left her there alive. He won't budge from it."

"Why would you expect him to admit it?" asked the elder McKell. "Don't murderers always deny their guilt?"

"Not as often as people think. Anyway, I've come to the conclusion that he's telling the truth."

"That's nonsense, Dad," Ellery said. "The man is guilty. I proved—"

"Maybe you didn't, son."

Ellery gaped at him.

"In any event, Inspector," growled Ashton McKell, "all this is your problem, not ours. Why have you brought Dane back into it?"

"Because he may be able to help us clear this up once and for all.

"Let's go back over this," the old man said in a head-on, plodding sort of way. And he ticked off the time elements of the crime. Sheila Grey had sent Ashton away at a few minutes past ten—at 10:03 P.M. Then she had sat down and written her letter about Dane to the police. "We've had people write out the letter in

177

longhand, as she did, trying to write the writing at the pace she must have used—it was fresh on her mind, a matter of urgency and fear, so she couldn't have written slowly.

"Five policewomen tried it. The quickest time ran a few seconds over four minutes, the longest just under six. Let's take the longest time. She had to go to her desk after you left, Mr. McKell, she had to sit down, take paper and pen from her drawer, write—and let's even say she read the letter over, which she may not have done—seal it in the first envelope, write on it 'To be opened in the event I die of unnatural causes,' place the first envelope into the larger envelope, and write on that, 'For the Police.'

"Now we've gone all through this, and no matter how we figure it, she simply couldn't have taken more than ten minutes at the outside for the whole procedure. I think ten minutes is way over—eight would be far more likely. But let's even call it ten. So she was finished with the letter and the sealing and so on by 10:13 at the latest. But she was shot at 10:23. What happened during those ten minutes? Okay, the killer came. But did it take him ten minutes to get the revolver out of the bedroom drawer and shoot her?"

"They talked," Dane suggested.

"And she picked up the phone and called the precinct with the killer standing over her? It won't wash. Remember what she said to the operator—that it was an emergency. When she got the precinct sergeant, she told him, 'Someone is in my apartment,' and you'll recall he said she was whispering, as if she didn't want to be overheard. No, she didn't spend any of the time talking to the murderer. Still—there it is. We don't have a full picture of that ten minutes, between the time she finished the letter and the shot the sergeant heard over the phone."

"I don't understand what's bugging you, Dad," Ellery said testily. "It's simple. Part of the ten minutes was consumed by Ramon's coming in and shooting her. The rest of it was just nothing—before he came she sat there, or worked on a sketch, or did something else inconsequential but time-consuming."

"But Ramon got there, he says, at 10:15," Inspector

Queen retorted. "He insists he only stayed four to five minutes at the most. That would bring us to, say, 10:20. If Ramon is telling the truth, there was enough time for somebody else to get into the penthouse after he left."

"If he's telling the truth," remarked Ellery caustically. "Or if his calculation of the time was accurate, which seems highly unlikely to me. What was he doing, holding a stopwatch on himself? We're dealing with minutes, Dad, not hours! I don't know what's the matter with you today."

The Inspector said nothing.

And Ellery looked at him very hard indeed. "And another thing," he said. "Ramon denies killing her. Did he say what he *was* doing up there?"

"Collecting a blackmail payment."

"What!"

"Ramon was blackmailing Sheila, too?" Ashton cried.

"That's right. He was playing both sides of the street."

"But why should Sheila have paid him money?"

"He says because of you, Mr. McKell. She didn't care about her reputation, but she did about yours, and she was willing to pay Ramon to keep his mouth shut."

Ashton fell silent.

"Incidentally, she was smarter than you were," the old man said dryly. "Ramon says she figured out right off that he was the blackmailer—that he'd probably followed you one Wednesday to find out what you were doing those afternoons and evenings, and learned that you were visiting her apartment in disguise. But she paid him anyway, to protect you."

Dane's father turned away. Lutetia's profile set. But then it softened, and she leaned over and took her husband's hand.

"Anyway, Ramon says he came up that night to put a harder squeeze on. He was collecting a thousand a month from her, too, but he was losing the money on the horses a lot faster than he was raking it in from you people, and he was leery about tackling you for more, Mr. McKell, figuring that a woman would be a softer touch. So he went to her. He says she was lying spread out in a chair looking pretty sick, half unconscious, hold-

179

ing her throat. She hardly seemed to know he was there, he said. He suspected something was very wrong and he beat it. But not before he spotted the letter addressed to the police in her handwriting, thought there might be something juicy in it for him, and put it in his pocket. That's his story, and I believe him."

"How did he leave the apartment?" Ellery asked in a half snarl. "By which door? Did he say?"

"The service door and service elevator."

"That would explain why Dane didn't run into him," began Ellery in a mutter; but then he subsided. No one said anything for a long time.

"I still don't see what all this has to do with me," Dane said finally.

The Inspector did not reply, and Ellery stirred and said, "It's true that if Sheila was that easy a mark for blackmail—and it shouldn't be too hard to trace thousand-dollar withdrawals from her account with dates Ramon ought to be able to supply—it isn't likely he would want to kill her . . . That would mean that my analysis of the crime was wrong—that the blackmailer was *not* the killer . . . It's because of the loose time situation . . . You're more than half inclined to think, then, that between 10:13 and 10:23 *two* people came to Sheila's apartment? Ramon the blackmailer, and then the killer? That Ramon did not shoot her?"

"I'm sure of it."

"Then why did Ramon run away," Judy burst out, "when Mr. Queen accused him of the shooting?"

"Blackmail isn't exactly a light rap, Miss Walsh," said Inspector Queen. "He panicked. Especially when, on top of it, he was accused of murder."

But Ellery was shaking his head and mumbling, more to himself than to them. "There's something awfully wrong here . . . We know how Sheila selected the names for her annual fashion collections. She did it consistently for seven consecutive years, making anagrams out of the names of her successive lovers. And this last one is Lady Norma, which is an anagram of Ramon. Is it possible 'Norma' came from some other name? 'Roman'? 'Moran'? I can't think of any others . . . Did you dig up another man in her life since Eddwin Odonnell, Dad?"

The Inspector shook his head.

"Then it still gets down to Ramon. He was more than Sheila's blackmailer, he was also her lover. And if he was her lover, she dropped him for Dane, and jealousy proved stronger than greed. In my book Ramon remains her killer."

"That's the funniest part of it," Inspector Queen said dryly, "if funny is the word. He says he wasn't ever her lover. At all."

"He says!" exploded Ellery. "I'm tired of hearing what Ramon says. He's lying!"

"Take it easy, son."

"He wasn't her lover?" Ashton McKell said, in a painfully relieved way.

And his son said, "I don't follow *any* of this."

"I don't blame you," the old policeman said, "It's one of those now-you-see-it-now-you-don't cases. But this is the one thing, Ellery, in which we don't have to take Ramon's word. We can prove it."

"That he was her lover," snapped Ellery, "or that he wasn't?"

"That he was not. The name on Sheila Grey's last finished drawing clinches it. When Ramon said he'd never had an affair with Sheila, we made a very careful laboratory examination of that sketch with the 'Lady Norma' on it. I don't know which method the lab used—sulfide of ammonia or ultraviolet rays—but whichever it was, the lab reports a positive finding. And what they found will stand up in any court of law.

"Underneath the words 'Lady Norma' on the sketch, they found another name."

Ellery had been through many ratiocinative crises in his life, but it was doubtful if any hit him as hard as his father's disclosure this bleak January afternoon. Perhaps the long weeks of inactivity in a hospital room, the sheer lack of tone in his muscles from too little exercise, had dulled the edge of his mental weapon, so that when the revelation came, its assault was all the more devastating. He felt as if he had been struck a powerful blow.

181

He shaded his eyes with his hand, his brain stumbling over the implications of the statement. Whatever the name was, it was obviously not Norma; therefore, Ramon had not inspired an anagram for the collection; therefore, there was no reason to postulate Ramon as Dane's predecessor in Sheila's affections; therefore, the chauffeur was telling the truth; therefore, blackmailer-as-murderer-also was out the window; and the blood, at least, was washed from Ramon's hands.

The murderer of Sheila Grey was someone else.

He had been completely wrong.

Completely!

Inspector Queen's dry voice broke into his sodden thoughts. "You see, someone had used ink eradicator—there was a bottle of it on Sheila's work desk—on the original collection name of the drawing, and then hand-printed 'Lady Norma' over the erasure. Notice I said 'hand*printed*'; because the name under 'Lady Norma' was hand*written*. And without any question we can establish the handwriting of the erased collection name as being Sheila Grey's."

"I didn't *see* an erasure," muttered Ellery. "Ink eradicator! I ought to go back to kindergarten. Dad, what was the name underneath in Sheila's writing?"

The Inspector reached into a portfolio and drew forth a photographic enlargement of the bottom portion of Sheila Grey's last finished drawing. He handed it to Ellery, and the others crowded about, pushing a little.

"Here it is," Ellery said, swallowing.

Two words in the now familiar Sheila Grey script stood out in the laboratory blowup through the printed 'Lady Norma,' like a ghost.

Lady Edna.

"Lady Edna," Ellery said with difficulty as the others stared, speechless. "Edna—*anagram of Dane.*"

"So she did intend to name her collection after you," Inspector Queen said to Dane, while Ellery fell into bitterest silence. "She must have done this before the argument that broke you up. And the drawing was lying there on her work desk that night. And with Ramon eliminated, who's the only other one we know was on or about the scene of the murder, and who also had motive

182

to erase the Dane anagram and substitute 'Norma' so as to throw suspicion on Ramon—can you tell us, Dane?"

Dane did not reply. His face was undergoing a dreadful transformation. Component features seemed to twist in incongruous directions at the same instant. His eyes burned with a feverish light. His hands clenched and unclenched and clenched again. A series of gibberish sounds began to growl in his throat.

Then Dane uttered a single maniacal cry and leaped at Inspector Queen's throat.

The attack was so sudden that the Inspector was taken by surprise. Before he could raise his hands, Dane's fingers were closing about the old man's throat and shaking the wiry body as if it were a puppy's.

Ellery staggered forward, but his legs betrayed him; he fell. In the end it was Dane's father who pitted brute strength against his son's and pulled him off the Inspector.

The old man lay back, gasping and clutching his throat.

As if an electrical contact had been broken, a current shut off, Dane went limp. He covered his face with his hands, and he wept.

"I can't stand it any more, I'm tired. I couldn't stay away from her. Judy? I'm sorry. Judy, Judy . . . Now you know what was wrong with me. It was driving me mad, what I had done to Sheila. It was bad enough that first time, when I almost strangled her. But when I lost my head again, later that awful night . . . I couldn't stay away, I came back. I told you I came back after walking and walking around outside. What I didn't tell you was that on my way back to the building I saw Ramon sneaking in—sneaking, unmistakably. Ramon—pussyfooting it up to Sheila's apartment through the service elevator . . . It came back to me then, those peculiar phone calls, her evasive remarks when I was around. Suppose those calls hadn't been from my father, as I'd thought? Suppose . . . suppose she was having an affair with Ramon? With my father's chauffeur, for God's sake! I went up after him, he didn't see me, because I used the front way. I was so quiet they didn't hear me. Ramon was talking in the workroom, with a mumble from Sheila now and then—I couldn't hear—I couldn't hear what they were saying—but it seemed to me he had an intimate note in his voice, and he laughed once or twice in a way . . . the way . . . I was sure they were lovers. Why else would he be there? It never occurred to me that he was blackmailing her. All I could think was, how vile, how cheap of her . . . He wasn't there long, but I heard him say he'd be back, and I took it to mean he was coming back to spend the night with her and I was so crazy blind furious with jealousy and humiliation I was shaking all over. And the fury got me. And I made my hands stop shaking—I didn't give a damn about Ramon, he didn't count, he was a bug, it was Sheila, Sheila . . . So I got the gun out of the drawer, my hands weren't shaking any more, and I went to the doorway of the workroom and she was sitting at her desk talking into the phone and I fired straight at her lying, cheating heart, and she fell over, and the phone fell out of her hand and I went over and picked it up and put it back on the cradle . . . And there was one other thing. I know how she named her collections because she had told me, she had shown me the one she'd finished for this year with my name on it in the anagram form of 'Edna.' The spell had passed and I was thinking cold sober and I knew that name mustn't be found because if it was, someone might figure out that 'Edna' meant me and that I was her current lover or had been, and so I looked over the sketches on her work desk and found the finished one with 'Edna' on it. I didn't dare destroy it, because there was probably a record of such a finished drawing at her salon that a lot of people knew about, so instead I went to work on it with ink eradicator and I applied it to the 'Lady Edna' so the name disappeared. Then I got an idea. It might well happen that I'd be suspected. Suppose I put a name down on the sketch, an anagram, that would lead the police astray. If they didn't see it, I could always call it to their attention . . . I had seen in a flash that an anagram could be made from Ramon's name. I never doubted he was her lover, never, not once—and, well, Ramon *had* been in the apartment only a few minutes before, and I was furious with him . . . I framed him with the anagram 'Lady Norma,' handprinting it over the erasure—I had no time to try to forge Sheila's handwriting. The whole thing didn't take me three minutes . . . Dad, Mother, Judy, I'm sorry, I'm sorry, there's something wrong inside me, there always has been, since I was a kid. Everything went wrong. First, Dad, you were accused. I'd never thought that would happen. Then you, Mother—that was terrible. Oh, you have to believe that I wouldn't ever have allowed either of you to be convicted. If everything else had failed, if Queen hadn't come up with something, if the bartender hadn't been found or the TV thing hadn't come out, I would have come forward and given myself up, I would have. You have to believe that. I would have confessed . . .

"Sheila, Sheila!"

About the Author

The team of FREDERIC DANNAY and MANFRED B. LEE —who, as everyone knows, are Ellery Queen—has written 71 books, including those first published under the pseudo-pseudonym of Barnaby Ross, and has edited 57 more. A conservative estimate has placed their total sales in various editions at more than 80,000,000 copies. And millions of listeners agreed when *TV Guide* awarded the Ellery Queen program its National Award as the best mystery show of 1950. Ellery Queen has won five annual "Edgars" (the national Mystery Writers of America awards similar to the "Oscars" of Hollywood), including the Grand Master award of 1960, and both the silver and gold "Gertrudes" awarded by Pocket Books.

Ellery Queen's most recent successes are *And On the Eighth Day* and *The Player on the Other Side*. He is internationally known as an editor—*Ellery Queen's Mystery Magazine* celebrated its 24th anniversary in 1965. His library of first editions (which is now at the University of Texas) contained the finest collection of books and manuscripts of detective short stories in the world.

These facts about Queen may account for the remark by Anthony Boucher, in his profile of Manfred B. Lee and Frederic Dannay, that "Ellery Queen *is* the American detective story."